# No One Else

Developmental Concepts, Inc.
8150 W. Emerald, Suite 100
Boise, ID  83704

Book design by:
Arbor Services, Inc.
www.arborservices.co/

Printed in the United States of America

*No One Else*
M.K. Tracy


1. Title 2. Author 3. Fiction


Library of Congress Control Number: 2017912396
ISBN 13: 978-0-692-93321-3

# No One Else

M.K. Tracy

*This book is dedicated to*
*My Three Loves*

# Contents

# Chapter 1

◇◇◇◇◇◇◇◇◇◇

A woman's wedding day should be the happiest day of her life. That's what they all said—all the bridal magazines, the romance novels, the movies. Just the word *wedding* evoked visions of a stunning bride in a white gown staring tearfully into her lover's eyes and gasping those eight clichéd and dramatic words: *this is the happiest day of my life*. But for Hannah Lund, it happened to be true.

*No*, Hannah corrected herself. *I'm not Hannah Lund anymore. I'm Hannah Martin now.* The thought brought a smile to her face, and she glanced around the room once more. The reception was the culmination of all the time she'd spent over the last few months clipping photos from magazines, pinning images on Pinterest, calling caterers, booking musicians, and visiting reception sites.

Gavin had jokingly dubbed her the CEO of the wedding, and now all the fruits of her efforts were laid out before her. The venue itself was an expansive room replete with luxurious woods, sleek stone, and at the far end, a set of glass doors that had been retracted to reveal a spectacular view of the river and the Sacramento skyline. She admired the tall, freestanding vases full of white lilies along the room's walls; the centerpieces of white roses and lavender blossoming from their little handblown glass vases; and the waiters bustling along with almost military efficiency in their tailored, dark-gray blazers. Heavenly background music hummed from the string quartet, its sound woven through with the chatting and laughing of party guests and the clinking of forks on plates. She could smell the mingled perfumes of the bridesmaids to her left rising above the heavier but equally pleasant odors of prime rib, pan-seared whitefish, au gratin potatoes, and freshly baked ciabatta rolls.

All these details she'd worked so painstakingly to choose and perfect washed over her, and she struggled to grasp them, to hang on to them. Already the evening seemed to be slipping by so fast.

With that thought, she glanced at the clock, and when she did she started and nearly knocked over her glass of champagne. It was time to cut the cake. As much as she'd tried to make herself sit back and enjoy the evening, the role of CEO was a difficult one to give up, apparently.

With a smile she reached over and took Gavin's strong, perfect hand. "Cake time," she said.

"Let's do this," he agreed and rose from his seat.

As they made their way across the room, Hannah's eyes kept returning to the man who was now her husband. She could not have found a more perfect mate even if she'd had the chance to build him from scratch. Gavin Martin was tall with the sculpted cheekbones of a runway model and the chiseled abs, emerald green eyes, and neatly cut blond hair to match. He'd been the backup center for the

UC Davis basketball team and about to graduate with his degree in business when they'd met a little more than three years ago.

Hannah had been a barista at a coffee shop called Mean Beans that spring, working her way through school to earn her bachelor's degree in social work. It had been a week of long work hours and grueling finals, but the minute she'd seen Gavin walk in the door, all her exhaustion had seemed to disappear.

"What'll you have?" she'd asked him smoothly as he walked up to the counter. A voice inside her couldn't help but hope he'd answer, "You."

In fact, he got a skinny vanilla latte with soy. She watched him throughout her shift as he studied, sitting alone at a corner table, and before she left she broke her cardinal rule, one she had never violated ever since that tragic Sadie Hawkins dance in sixth grade: she asked Gavin Martin out. She could still remember the cocky little grin he'd given her, the glint in his sly green eyes.

"Sure," he'd said quietly, but his body language had said, *What took you so long to ask?* His self-confidence was an incredible turn-on. Even now, with all her friends and family watching, she could feel a feverish heat rising to her cheeks just thinking about it.

Three years and two months later, here they were.

Now, moving through the room with Gavin at her side, she felt like she was floating. It was hard to corral the train of her dress as she made her way through the crowd, and she made a mental note to pick out a simpler dress next time she got married. That was a little inside joke she and Gavin shared. "Next time I get married,

I'm eloping," he'd say when wedding planning got hectic, and they'd both laugh. Gavin was so funny sometimes.

They stood before the table where the cake sat. Like most details about the wedding, the cake was traditional but with a modern edge. A tiered white cake with white frosting, it was square rather than round and traced with swirling, silvery accents. It didn't seem right to eat something silver, but the lady at the bakery had assured them it was perfectly safe.

Hannah picked up the big, mother-of-pearl-handled knife and placed it on the cake. Gavin, however, had been distracted by one of his drunken basketball buddies and exchanged gestures with him. Hannah didn't know what he was communicating to his buddy, and judging from past experience she was pretty sure she didn't want to know. She elbowed Gavin, getting his attention.

"You have to put your hand on mine when we cut the cake," she said.

"Why? It takes two people to cut through a cake?"

"It's just what you do, Gavin," she said.

With a shrug he put his hand on hers and began to press down, but Hannah had to stop him. The photographer was still making her way over through the crowd. She was a black-clad New Yorker with a blonde bob and a huge lens on her camera that seemed, to Hannah, like overkill. She looked like she should be shooting photos of the Super Bowl or wild geese in flight, not a simple wedding. What was the woman's name? Candice? In the rush and blur of the moment, she had trouble remembering.

"Okay, *now*," Hannah said when everything was ready, and they cut the cake together.

After some careful slicing, they each had a square of cake in their hands, ready to feed to one another. From the look on Gavin's face, she could imagine what he was thinking: *Why on earth is this a tradition? Feeding each other cake? What does it have to do with anything?*

She reassured him with a smile, which elicited a round of applause from the crowd. Aunts hooted and clapped, cousins chuckled, and a few of Gavin's drunk former teammates chanted, "Eat it, eat it!"

"I won't make a mess if you won't," Gavin told Hannah.

She smiled. She'd always thought brides and grooms violently jamming cake into each other's mouths was gross. Of course he'd think the tradition was stupid too. It was one more way they were meant for each other.

"On three," Candice the photographer barked. If Hannah was the CEO of the wedding reception, the photographer seemed to think she was the czar. It irritated Hannah, but she kept a placid smile on her face.

"One, two . . . three!" Candice said.

Hannah gently fed her bite to Gavin; he jammed his in her face. She felt the frosting smear all over her upper lip, some of it worming its way up her nose. She almost choked on the part that went into her mouth, coughing for a moment before she managed to chew and swallow it. Gavin laughed. Everyone laughed. And after a split second of shock, Hannah did too. She waited until Gavin looked the other way then scooped a frosting rose off the cake and jammed it into his ear. The reception-goers erupted into another bout of laughter. People were having a good time. Clearly the open bar was paying off.

"All right," Gavin said, digging the frosting out of his ear with a napkin. "Well played, Mrs. Martin."

Hearing the name made her smile.

"Truce?" he asked.

"Truce," she agreed, and they exchanged a kiss, eliciting another cheer from the crowd. Then she excused herself to the bathroom, where she spent the next ten minutes blowing frosting out of her nose.

•   •   •

Upon her return, Hannah was relieved to find that her carefully mapped-out plan was being executed in her absence. The spreadsheet clearly stated that after the cake was cut, dance music would replace the string quartet. DJ Jazzy Chuck had set up his equipment, and now, precisely just as the plan prescribed, dance music blared from a set of massive speakers while the string musicians packed up their instruments. Hannah felt a smile of contentment cross her face: as wonderful as the day was, nothing made her feel quite as good as knowing she'd made a plan and executed it to perfection. She wove her way through the sea of guests, accepting well wishes, shaking hands, and exchanging hugs as she headed toward the dance floor.

Most of the bridesmaids were out there now, dancing their tails off and rapping about how they liked big butts. Hannah was sure Tara, her maid of honor, had once again taken her post seriously and led the charge to get the party started. Sure enough, Hannah spotted her a moment later right in the middle of the action.

Tara and Hannah had been roommates freshman year at UC Davis. Despite some early spats about things like whether or not to allow guys to spend the night in the room and who used whose deodorant, the two had become best friends.

She wasn't surprised to find Tara on the dance floor. What surprised her was finding Gavin there surrounded by the bridesmaids. They frolicked around him, shaking and gyrating, obviously trying to make him blush and hamming it up for the crowd of jolly, half-inebriated family members. Gavin didn't seem to be blushing, though. He smiled and bounced to the beat in the macho, stone-footed way that—for him—passed for dancing. Meanwhile Tara worked him over with some of her signature moves. The sight of the two of them having fun together filled Hannah with joy, and she laughed out loud. Gavin was always such a good sport; it was nice of him to play along.

She was about to wade her way onto the dance floor to join them when a voice from behind startled her.

"So, no daddy-daughter dance?"

Hannah turned to find her father standing behind her with her stepmom, Trudy. Prior to the wedding she hadn't seen them for eight months, and she'd even toyed with the idea of not inviting them. Now, even amid the festivities, the two looked as gloomy and ornery as ever.

"Gavin and I decided not to have a father-daughter dance or the dollar dance," Hannah said. "We thought it seemed weird to try to extort money from our friends."

That was why they'd skipped the dollar dance. She didn't explain why they'd opted out of the daddy-daughter dance. She figured if he didn't understand by then, he never would.

Her father nodded coldly.

"Well, congratulations," Trudy said with the vaguely Southern accent of hers that made Hannah want to cringe. The voice brought up too many bad memories, first of her parents' divorce, then of the sad, lonely time she'd spent living with her father and his cruel new wife after her mother's death.

"Looks like you found yourself a good man," Trudy said. "A better one than you deserve, I suspect."

Hannah forced a fake smile onto her face. "Thanks, Trudy," she said flatly. She surveyed the woman's sequined top and was tempted to say, "Nice shoulder pads" but decided to take the high road.

Instead she mumbled, "I'm glad you guys came. Excuse me," and walked away.

Despite the difficulty in having them there, she took comfort in knowing she was marrying a man who was nothing like her father, and if—no, *when*—she and Gavin had kids, they would never, ever have to suffer through the heartbreak of divorce as she had. That was a vow she'd made to herself long ago; the wedding vows she'd made today were only a confirmation of it.

Out on the dance floor, she found Gavin and Tara still dancing together. She was impressed that Tara was able to move so well with a champagne flute in her hand, without spilling a drop. *Practice makes perfect*, Hannah thought as she danced her way up to them.

As soon as Tara caught sight of Hannah approaching, she gave a little scream of excitement and hugged her.

"Oh my God, girl, I cannot believe you're actually married!" she gushed, clearly a bit buzzed.

"I know," Hannah said.

Tara suddenly became very serious. "Listen, I just want to say that . . . I know I was a bitch when you two first got together. It's just that Gavin is amazing. I mean, he's hot, he's tall, he's sweet, he's funny, charming . . . The truth is, I think all our friends had a little bit of a crush on him."

Hannah smiled, nodding. When Tara was drunk and ranting, it was always best to indulge her.

"The truth is," Tara continued, "I was jealous. And I'm sorry."

Hannah laughed and embraced her friend. "It's okay, Tara. I love you. You'll always be my best friend. And we're going to find you someone as hot as Gavin, I swear."

When they disengaged, Tara's serious mood was gone. She downed the rest of her drink in a gulp and danced with Hannah for a moment until she caught sight of a tall, handsome cousin of Gavin's across the hall and danced off to find him.

Finally Hannah made her way into her husband's arms.

"Well, it looks like you made quite an impression on the bridesmaids," she said with a laugh.

"I know. They were swarming me," Gavin said. "Thanks for coming to my rescue, Mrs. Martin."

Hannah smiled so big it made her cheeks hurt. "Anytime, Mr. Martin," she said.

Just then a slow song came on, and she let herself relax into his arms, swaying in time with the music. With her eyes closed and her body pressed against his, she floated in the warm embrace of a nighttime sea.

# Chapter 2

"Quinn, Sage, take the dress off your brother, please," Hannah said, glancing up from the desk den where she sat paying bills. The two little girls only squealed with laughter as their little brother, Beau, cruelly dressed in a pink ballerina's outfit, took a few tottering steps then fell back on his diapered bum and sat looking around as if mildly confused.

For Hannah, the seven years since her wedding had slipped past in a blur. Only three months after the big day, she had learned she was pregnant with her first child, a baby girl she and Gavin had named Quinn. The pregnancy had come as a bit of a happy surprise—they hadn't exactly been trying to have a baby, but they hadn't been trying not to either.

Gavin had been pounding the pavement, networking and submitting resumes, hoping to land a job as a pharmaceutical rep. When they learned that Quinn was on the way, however, he accepted the first job he was offered, as an outside salesman for an industrial supply company. Hannah had intended to get a job too, but they decided to put those plans on hold until baby Quinn was old enough to go to

11

day care. It was important to Gavin that Hannah stay home to take care of the baby, and it was important to Hannah too.

Hannah spent the months of her pregnancy reading parenting books and wondering at her swelling feet, expanding breasts, and ballooning belly and the other strange changes her body was going through. Meanwhile Gavin was out peddling pipes, valves, and fittings to contractors, factories, and distributors throughout Northern California and Oregon.

He was gone a lot, which was hard for Hannah. She missed him when he was gone and felt much better on the weekends when he was at home. Fortunately Gavin seemed not to mind the travelling, the nights spent in hotels, or the lonely dinners eaten on the road.

Soon enough baby Quinn entered the world. She was a happy, healthy, perfect child. Gavin was on the road in Redding when she came, but as soon as he got the call he hurried back to Sacramento to meet his little girl, and he seemed as thrilled with her as Hannah was.

As Quinn grew up, she continued to be perfect. She was sweet, intelligent, and eager to please, and Hannah felt like her heart overflowed with love for her blossoming family.

With a baby to take care of, time seemed to go by even faster. Now, as she looked up from the stack of bills next to her laptop, Hannah felt as if she had blinked and woken up six years later with a second daughter, Sage, and a little son. Beau was a blissfully eager and energetic two-year-old with a head full of dark ringlets that Hannah couldn't bring herself to have cut. Sage, at five, was a precocious little firecracker with the same pretty, wildly curly hair as her brother. Quinn, at seven, was their ringleader and all-wise big sister. She was slender and tall with long, straight, sandy-blonde hair like her father's.

"Make him wear the tiara!" Sage shrieked happily as she adjusted the ruffle on poor little Beau's pink skirt.

"No," Quinn said thoughtfully. "I'm going to go get a bonnet from my Cabbage Patch doll. That'll be funnier."

Just then the front door opened, and the kids all froze, exchanging excited glances.

"Hello?" came a familiar voice from the foyer.

"Daddy!" Sage shouted, and the girls stampeded toward the front door with little Beau toddling along behind them, clutching a sippy cup in one hand.

Hannah entered the amount for the cable bill, clicked submit, and hurried out of the den. She found Gavin sitting on the couch under a pile of kids. Sage was hugging him, Quinn was telling him about a school project, and Beau was trying to shove the end of Gavin's tie into his mouth.

"Hey, hon. I'd give you a kiss if I could get to you," Hannah said, settling into a chair.

"Later," Gavin said with a wink. Hannah was grateful that he was always chipper when he came home. *The road agrees with him*, she thought. It reminded her of some smutty romance novel, of a cowboy coming home to see his woman after a long time on the range, and for some reason the thought was a bit of a turn-on. She glanced at her watch and did a quick calculation, counting the number of hours left until bedtime.

"Listen, why don't you kids go and play in the den for a minute, okay? I have to talk to Mommy," Gavin said.

Sage looked disappointed, but Quinn, as always, was eager to please.

"Do you want me to put your briefcase away, Daddy?" she asked.

"Sure, by the desk," he said. Quinn picked up the briefcase and hurried into the other room. Sage made a pouty face and slid off Gavin's lap. She grabbed her little brother under the arms in something that looked to Hannah like a professional-wrestling move.

"C'mon, Beau. Mommy and Daddy have to *talk*," Sage said as if she weren't very happy about it. Although the way Sage lugged Beau didn't look very comfortable, he giggled happily as she dragged him from the room.

When they were alone, Gavin looked at Hannah.

"Well, you want the good news or the bad news?" he asked.

Hannah felt her good mood deflating, replaced by fear.

"The bad," she said quietly.

Gavin pursed his lips. "I got laid off," he said.

Hannah took a few seconds to process what he was saying. "What? Why?"

Gavin shrugged. "I don't know. Downsizing. They're shifting to more inside sales and Internet business. On-the-road guys like me aren't where the future is, according to management."

Hannah suddenly felt cold, as if all the blood were draining from her body. She thought of the bills she'd paid today and the other ones that still had to be paid. They had the mortgage, Quinn's dance lessons, the car payments . . . Even in good months, when Gavin's commissions were high, it was hard to make ends meet. But now?

"What are we going to do?" she asked.

Gavin shook his head. "Don't worry, babe. We'll figure something out. What's for dinner? I'm starving."

"Wait," Hannah said. "You said there was bad news and good news. What's the good news?"

Gavin smiled his charming smile, but with a little sadness in it now. "Sorry, babe. I'm still trying to come up with some," he said.

• • •

Half an hour later, Hannah was scrambling to make Gavin's favorite dinner: spaghetti with her special homemade white sauce. Since she hadn't planned on making it tonight, she was missing a few ingredients, but she made a couple of substitutions she thought would go unnoticed. She felt so bad for Gavin, she really wanted him to have a special dinner.

Unfortunately things didn't go quite as she'd hoped. Hannah dug through the cabinet to find the garlic salt for the sautéed chicken that would top the pasta, but she couldn't find it, only garlic powder, which she knew from bitter experience was not at all the same thing. While her nose was in the cabinet, the girls screamed wildly in the living room as they played their favorite video game, Dance Magic USA. They both knew all the moves and were cute to watch, but they sometimes got so fired up when they played it, their laughter grew a bit too shrill to be endurable.

"Girls, calm down, or I'm shutting it off," she called mildly. Wasn't Gavin watching them?

Hannah decided some Cajun seasoning mixed with Italian herbs would have to do in place of the garlic salt tonight. She'd just begun to sprinkle it on the chicken when little Beau came waddling in, crying. With one look at his gait and one sniff of the putrid air surrounding him, she knew at once what the problem was: a dirty diaper. She picked him up to take him over to the changing table in his room, but when she glanced back, she found the pot full of spaghetti about to boil over.

"Shi—shish kabobs," she said. Converting curse words into more -benign phrases had become a talent of Hannah's over the last few years, but somehow the new expletives just weren't as satisfying as the real thing. After checking to make sure Beau was safely out of scalding range, she yanked the saucepan off the burner, but not in time to keep it from boiling over and flooding the stovetop with white froth.

Beau was screaming now, tugging on her pant leg as she turned the heat down and placed the pan back on the burner. The timer went off. Time to take the rolls out.

"Gavin!" she called. "Can you change Beau's diaper, please? I'm in the middle of making dinner."

"Busy," Gavin called back.

"He's busy," she said to the pot of spaghetti, which was boiling over once again. She turned the burner down fuarther.

"Busy doing what, honey?" she called, trying to keep the irritation out of her voice.

"Online," he called back, sounding impatient and distracted. The girls' laughter squealed from the living room once again. Beau squalled.

Hannah took a deep, steadying breath, trying to let the rising tide of anger inside her abate. What was wrong with her? So Gavin was online. He was probably looking for a new job. This had to be one of the hardest days of his life. She needed to support him.

Pushing her annoyance aside, she shouted to the girls once more: "Quieter, please. Daddy is working on the computer." She glanced at the rolls in the oven, decided they needed a few more minutes, and put the chicken in its skillet on a burner at a low temperature so it would start to cook without burning. She checked the pasta once more, then scooped Beau up and carried him toward his bedroom.

On the way down the hall, she heard Gavin's laughter coming from the office and paused to stick her head in.

"What?" she asked. She couldn't imagine what could possibly be that funny on CareerPlace.com.

"The dog hits the guy right in the nuts." Gavin chuckled. "Watch!"

Hannah watched and, sure enough, in the YouTube video Gavin played for her, a basset hound head butted his owner right in the most private of places.

Maybe it was the smell of Beau's diaper, which suddenly made her want to gag. Maybe it was the scent coming from the kitchen, where the rolls were now starting to burn. Maybe it was the sound of the girls who, unsupervised in the living room, were squealing once more. Maybe the nagging thought that they had only enough money in the bank to cover one more mortgage payment. But somehow Hannah did not want to laugh. She felt more like crying.

"What? That's not funny?" Gavin asked. He seemed hurt that she didn't like the video.

"It's great, Gavin," she said sarcastically. "I can see how busy you are. I'll change Beau's diaper myself."

# Chapter 3

Less than a month after Gavin lost his job, Hannah woke up in bed alone. Lately she'd been waking up earlier than Gavin and completing the morning rituals of dressing Beau, making breakfast, preparing lunches, and dropping the girls off at school all before he even rolled out of bed.

She figured it had to be the stress of losing his job. He was understandably depressed, and she knew that depressed people had a hard time getting out of bed—like that guy from the Beach Boys, Brian Wilson.

The fact that Gavin was awake now gave her a little shot of adrenaline. Had he gotten a call about an interview he hadn't told her about? Was it meant to be a surprise? Or maybe he'd already gotten a job. Maybe he would come home at five o'clock wearing a suit and carrying a bouquet of flowers, surprising her by offering her a business card that read "Gavin Martin, VP of Sales."

The idea of Gavins getting back on track and ending their financial stress made her heart beat faster, and as much as she'd have liked a surprise, she wanted immediate good news more. As the bills mounted and the creditors started calling, it wasn't just that she wanted something good to happen—she needed it. And so she sprang out of bed, grabbed her robe from the bedpost, and hurried down the stairs, hoping to find Gavin before he left.

He wasn't in the kitchen or in the office. Not in the living room either.

"Gavin?" she called. Out in the garage, she heard a voice—someone talking. She opened the door and found Gavin walking toward the trunk of his car, talking into a Bluetooth headset. He wore khakis and a blue-and-white striped polo shirt, and his golf clubs were slung over his shoulder.

"Yeah, right. The day you shoot a sixty-nine, they'll be building an igloo in hell." He dropped the clubs into the trunk of his Nissan Maxima and then shut it. As he headed to the driver's seat, he felt Hannah's questioning eyes on him and looked up.

"Hey, babe. What's up?" he asked, clamping two fingers over the voice receiver.

"I thought you were looking for jobs today," Hannah said. The strength seemed to have left her body suddenly, and it had left her voice too. In her own ears, she sounded weary, exhausted.

Gavin shrugged. "I will. After I play eighteen," he said.

With that he got into the car and shut the door. He pushed the button on the remote clipped to the sun visor, and the garage door groaned its way upward. Hannah stood stiffly in the doorway, watching as Gavin backed the car out of the garage.

She could hear his conversation trailing behind him from the car's open sunroof.

"You've lost it, man. I'll bet you fifty bucks you don't outdrive me all day . . . Yeah? You're on."

He gave Hannah a little wave as he reached the bottom of the driveway, then, with a little squawk of the tires, he was gone.

• • •

At one o'clock1:00 p.m. Hannah held Beau against her hip as she bustled around the kitchen preparing his lunch. Dr. Phil was on the TV, and the large, bald psychologist was berating a young husband for cheating on his teenage wife.

"You've got to take some responsibility!" he kept saying in his yawning Southern drawl.

Normally Hannah found daytime TV beyond depressing and never watched it, but today she felt the need for distraction. Gavin wasn't back from his golf outing yet. With every tick of the clock's minute hand, she felt her blood pressure rising. The higher it got, the harder she tried to talk herself out of being angry. Sure, she would have preferred Gavin to be working a little harder at finding a new job. And sure, she found it really irritating that he was spending what precious little money they had left on a round of golf while she was left at home with the kids. But stewing about it wasn't going to improve the situation, so she tried to concentrate on other things.

"We're just keeping busy, aren't we, little muffin?" she said to Beau as she put his dish of macaroni and cheese into the microwave to heat up. As she did, she glanced out the window at the girls, who were playing on the swing set. At least they were happy, she thought, and she wished—not for the first time—she could spent just one more blissful hour as a kid, without any grown-up worries to stress her out.

"It's going to be okay, Beau," she said to her son in a distracted, sing-song voice. "Yes it is!"

"Id-ih!" Beau said, agreeing with her.

"It is, yes it is," she said and smiled. Oddly the toddler's encouragement made her feel better.

*That's how far gone I am*, she thought, amused with herself.

The microwave counted down to its final beep—twenty-five seconds to go, twenty-four, twenty-three, and then it stopped. The green digital numbers disappeared. The humming ceased.

She glanced at the TV. The screen was a flat gray color, and Dr. Phil's voice had cut off in midsentence.

"What on earth?" she said aloud and made a quick march through the house, checking for appliance "on" lights and flipping light switches. The electricity in the living room and the dining room were out too.

"Is it the whole neighborhood?" she asked Beau as if he would know.

Peering out the front window, she couldn't tell if anyone else's power was out since it was daylight. But it certainly wasn't windy, and there didn't seem to be any bad weather that could have knocked down a power line.

On her way back through the house, she could barely see. The day was gloomy and overcast, and she found it difficult to see inside the parts of the house without windows. On the way to the kitchen, she stubbed her toe on the coatrack in the hall and had to bite her lip to keep from yelling "ow" in poor little Beau's ear. After hobbling into the kitchen, she glanced out the window at the girls once more and then paused, drumming her fingers on the counter.

She thought of one possibility for the power outage that she'd hadn't checked, but the thought of it made her stomach feel like a rubber band pulled too tight. After a moment's hesitation, she went to the pantry, took out a flashlight, and still carrying Beau, made her way into the dimly lit office. The blinds were shut, so she opened them and rummaged through Gavin's desk until she found the folder marked "bills." Under the tab for "electric bills," she pulled out a small stack of pages. Her eyes scanned them, one after another. A few words popped out at her: "LATE," "URGENT," "DISCONNECT NOTICE."

The final bill was printed on ominous, pinkish-red paper and was marked with a disconnect date that had passed three days ago. Beneath that she read a paragraph stating that if a customer's power were shut off, it might take as long as three days to get it turned back on, and then it would happen only after they'd paid their past-due balance plus a reconnection fee and a $200 deposit.

The bill shivered in her trembling hand, and she eased herself down into Gavin's leather office chair to avoid collapsing to the ground and possibly hurting Beau. They had no power. They had no money to pay the power bill. Instead of looking for a job, Gavin was off having fun. Hannah couldn't go get a job because if she did, who would look after the kids? She was alone.

Despite her best efforts, Hannah felt her face contracting, her lips trembling. For the first time since she'd married Gavin more than seven years ago, she sobbed.

Beau grabbed at her face, his chubby fingers slipping off her tear-slick cheeks, but looking at him only made Hannah feel worse. She couldn't even heat up his lunch now. The situation was desperate. What were they going to do?

She sat in the dimly lit room crying, and in a few minutes Beau slipped off to sleep.

Perhaps ten minutes later, Hannah's phone beeped in the pocket of her sweater. Moving carefully to avoid waking Beau, she dug it out. She hoped the text would be from Gavin, saying he was on his way home, but it wasn't. It was from Tara.

The text would change Hannah's life forever.

# Chapter 4

Gavin didn't return home until nearly four o'clock in the afternoon. Hannah lay on the living room floor playing Chutes and Ladders with the girls with one hand and cradling Beau with her other arm when she heard his car pull into the driveway. She watched as her husband entered, slipped wordlessly through the kitchen, and hurried toward the stairs.

"Hi," she said, getting his attention.

"Hey, babe. Just grabbing a shower real quick. Eighteen holes—you work up a sweat!" he said and continued toward the staircase.

"Wait," Hannah said, setting Beau on the carpeted floor and rising. "I got a text today from Tara. She offered me a job."

Gavin frowned. "What do you mean?"

"A job. You know, clock in, do work, clock out, get a paycheck?" She was angry that the power was shut off and upset that Gavin had left her alone all day. The best way to diffuse her frustration was with a joke.

Gavin, however, seemed more confused than amused.

"You can't get a job. What about the kids?"

"You can watch them until you get a job. Then we can get day care," Hannah said.

Gavin made a face like he was smelling someone's dirty sock. "I guess it might work—temporarily. Is it here in Sacramento, or is she still down in Stockton?"

Hannah hesitated. "Well, that's sort of the catch," she said. "It's in Hickory Bluff."

Gavin laughed. "Hickory Bluff? Where the hell is that?"

"I'll tell you where the *heck* it is," she said, glancing at the kids to make sure they weren't picking up on his bad language. They weren't; the girls were busy bopping Beau on the face with a couch pillow and making him laugh. "It's in Utah," she said, following Gavin up the stairs.

"You really want to uproot the whole family and move to Utah? Come on, Hannah." Gavin said as he stepped into the bathroom. He stripped off his golf shirt, revealing his muscle-rippled torso. As busy as the family was, he always seemed to find the time to work out.

"Yes, Gavin. If the choice is between starving to death in Sacramento and working at a respectable job in Podunk, Utah, then I'd rather move to Utah."

Gavin slipped his watch off his wrist and glanced at it as he set it on the counter. "Can we talk about this later? The guys are waiting for me at the Tiger Grill."

"Waiting for you for what? You've been with them all day!" Hannah said, her voice verging on a shout.

"A game is on tonight. I like to watch the game with my friends. You know this," Gavin said calmly, and he tried to turn on the bathroom light. It clicked, but nothing happened. "Light burn out?" he asked.

Hannah took a slow breath, trying to match his calmness with her own. "While you were out golfing, our electricity was shut off. Do you have any idea what it's like to try to entertain three kids all day with no electricity? I called, and you didn't even answer your cell phone."

Gavin rolled his eyes. "Have you ever seen a cell phone tower in the middle of a golf course?" he asked.

"That's not the point," Hannah said. "The point is, how are we going to get our electricity turned back on, Gavin?"

He turned on the water in the shower and held his fingers in the stream, waiting for it to get hot. "Maybe your dad will loan us some cash. You know he's got plenty," he said.

Hannah felt the final barrier that held back her anger crumbling. She was about to unleash on him as he slipped out of his boxers.

"Listen, baby, I'm sorry the power got turned off," he said. "And I'm sorry you were stuck here with the kids all day. One of the guys I'm going out with tonight owns an electrical supply business, and he might be hiring. If it goes well, maybe he'll offer me something. Plus I have that FedEx interview in a couple of days, remember? Something's going to work out, okay? We don't have to get drastic."

Just when Hannah had been about to explode, Gavin's apologies stole the fire from her anger. Suddenly she simply felt exhausted and scared.

"Okay," she said. "But if those things don't work out, we're going to consider the Utah thing seriously, okay?"

"Scout's honor," Gavin said, though Hannah knew he'd never been camping in his life. "Meanwhile, I guess, we'll be living by candlelight. It's pretty warm in here. There's room for two," he teased, hitting her with that charming grin.

Despite her anger, fear, and frustration, a small smile crossed Hannah's lips. She moved toward the shower door when a little voice from downstairs called up to her. It was Sage. "Mom! Quinn took my Barbie! Tell her to give it *back!*"

*Well, now we can add one more to my list of frustrations: sexual frustration.* She gave Gavin an apologetic glance as she backed away from him toward the bathroom door, but he'd already retreated into the shower and was shampooing his hair.

With a sigh, Hannah headed downstairs.

• • •

With no electricity, the dinner menu that night became pizza and salad. There were a lot of things in the refrigerator that Hannah would have liked to use up before they went bad, but she had no way to cook them on the electric stove—and she wasn't about to resort to cooking over a campfire.

She helped the kids make the best of it. They played flashlight tag, built couch-cushion forts in the living room, and read bedtime stories by candlelight. Quinn, being the oldest, asked her mother outright why the power was out. Fortunately she was still young enough to accept Hannah's evasive answer and, after a moment of skepticism, surrendered to the adventure of life without power as her younger brother and sister had done.

By nine o'clock the kids were all asleep, and Hannah was finally free to let the smile disappear from her face. Immediately she poured herself a much-needed glass of wine and headed to the home office. There she sat for many minutes, sipping the wine and looking over the family's dire finances in the flickering candlelight. Her family's well-being was as tenuous as that light, she realized. With one more gust of misfortune, it could be snuffed out. This month the power was out. Next month they might be facing foreclosure.

She took a long, slow slip of her wine, and her gaze drifted from the papers spread out in front of her to the cell phone that sat on the corner of her desk. She wished she could call Gavin, to hear his voice as he told her everything would be okay. But no; he wouldn't want to be bothered when he was out with his friends.

She picked up the phone for perhaps the tenth time that night, hoping to find a text saying Gavin's golf buddy had offered him the job. There was nothing.

Impulsively she scrolled through her contacts. When her father's name appeared, she lingered on it. *Ask your father for a loan*, Gavin had said.

Thoughts seeped into her mind like water through the hull of a sinking ship. In her memory she was twelve years old, eating a frozen dinner while *Jeopardy* played on the TV. Her father sat in the La-Z-Boy next to her eating his Stouffer's pot pie, every once in a while muttering the wrong answer to a question.

Hannah was the youngest of four kids. Her oldest brother was an insurance agent down in San Diego, the middle brother a blackjack dealer at the Tropicana in Las Vegas, and her sister the receptionist at a car dealership in Tempe, Arizona. They had all come to visit when Hannah's mother was diagnosed with cancer and had stayed for as long as they could. *The doctors are hopeful about her prognosis, but you'd better come see her anyway,* her father had told them on the phone. That had been six months earlier. They had bought cards and teddy bears, cooked dinners, and helped clean the house. In the end they could keep their lives on hold only for so long, and they'd left, leaving Hannah alone with her father and her sick mother.

Hannah watched as her mother lost her hair, her appetite, and a quarter of her weight. Before, she'd spent her days singing in the kitchen, baking cookies, driving her daughter to swim practice, helping with homework, and packing lunches. Now, she lay in her bed all day long, too weak to rise. She smelled different. Dark circles ringed her eyes. Her hands, which had once played Christmas carols on the piano in the corner of the living room, were now skeletal. Her bright, cheery voice had withered to a rasp.

Even though she looked and acted like a different person, Hannah knew that the woman sleeping in the den now was her mother—yet she could not quite stop herself from being afraid every time she went into that room. It wasn't her mother she was afraid of. It was the sudden change in her, the sickness. It was the idea that a person could be healthy and vivacious one day and on the verge of death the next. It was the unpredictability of the universe, the frailty of the human body, the moral chaos of undeserved suffering, and, most of all, the idea that her mother would soon be gone forever that troubled her. For all these reasons, she avoided going into that little den while her mother was dying, entering it only for specific reasons: to deliver soup or bring her mom a new blanket. She would feel guilty about it for the rest of her life.

Twelve-year-old Hannah stirred her mashed potatoes with her fork, staring at the TV without seeing it, listening to the show without hearing a word. Suddenly two sounds came at once. From the driveway outside the house came the honk of a car horn; from the darkness of the den, her mother's plaintive voice.

Hannah's dad looked at his watch and rose from the chair.

"Heat your mom up some food, okay?" he said. He was already at the closet taking out his coat.

"Where are you going?" Hannah asked.

"Gotta run some errands. I'll be back soon."

"I thought the car was broken."

"It is. That's my ride."

"Who?"

Another call from the bedroom. "Stan?"

Hannah's father ignored it. "I'll be back in a bit," he said and left, shutting the front door behind him.

Hannah watched from the window as her father climbed into the passenger seat of a big car. As it drove in reverse, she was suddenly flooded with terror. What if her mother died while she was alone with her? What would Hannah do? How would she save her?

Frantically she yanked open the door and ran out into the chill evening air, then stopped halfway down the driveway. The driver of the car stopped and looked at her. It was a woman, tall and blonde with a large mouth, coarse features, and red lipstick. Something in her cold stare gave Hannah a prickle of uneasiness. She did not speak or motion to Hannah; she merely looked at her for a moment and then turned away.

Twelve-year-old Hannah watched with tears on her cheeks as the car lurched into gear and drove off into the deepening night. Slowly she turned and walked back into the house.

Against the odds, Hannah's mother managed to beat her cancer into remission. Two weeks after the good news came, Hannah's father filed for divorce. Only then was Hannah finally introduced to the mystery driver. Her name was Trudy Bigelow, her father said. He was in love with her, and they were going to get married.

Less than a year after the wedding, Hannah's mother's cancer returned. This time she lasted only a few weeks. Hannah had no choice but to move in with her father and his new wife. She imagined at the beginning that her anger toward her father would lessen over time, but it did not. The experience was the first lesson in betrayal Hannah had ever known, and it was one she would never forget.

Now, in her candlelit den, she stared at her father's highlighted phone number on the screen of her phone for a long moment, then thrust it away. She set the phone on the edge of her desk, as far away as she could, and stared at it distrustfully. There was no way she would ask her father for help—not even if it meant she would have to starve to death.

She glanced over at the clock. It was almost eleven. Where had the time gone? So late, and Gavin still wasn't home. He hadn't even bothered to call.

The memories, the loneliness, and the stress all combined in Hannah's stomach like air, fire, and gasoline mixing in a car's engine, igniting and combusting—fueling her. Before she knew it, she was on her feet, snatching the cell phone from the desk and hurrying down the hall.

"Hey, Tara? It's me, Hannah. I want to talk to you some more about that job," she said as she hurried into the garage.

She grabbed some cardboard boxes, charged into the kitchen with them, and started to pack.

•  •  •

At a quarter after one in the morning, Hannah finally heard the groan of the garage door. A few moments later, Gavin entered the kitchen. His hair was a little disheveled, his clothing askew, his eyes unfocused, his balance slightly unsteady. All the changes were subtle, so much so that someone who didn't know him well might not even have noticed he was drunk, but Hannah did. She thought of commenting, then bit her tongue. The last thing in the world she wanted to be was a nagging wife—like her stepmother Trudy was.

"Hey, babe," Gavin said brightly, moving toward Hannah and then suddenly stopping. His smile disappeared as his eyes ranged around the room, taking in the open, empty cabinets, the neat stack of boxes in the corner, the packing tape on the kitchen island, all of it illuminated by candlelight.

He heaved a big sigh and dropped his keys on the counter. "Shit," he said wearily. "We're moving to Utah, aren't we?"

# Chapter 5

At ten o'clock on the following Sunday morning, the Martin family rolled into Hickory Bluff, Utah. Their Subaru Forester was so overloaded, its muffler nearly touched the ground, and the U-Haul trailer it pulled lurched along behind it like a pet elephant on a leash. The trip had been a grueling, eleven-hour drive across the wasteland of Northern Nevada, and Hannah was pretty sure if she had to listen to one more Pixar movie blaring from the backseat, she would lose what was left of her sanity. She was exhausted from packing, stressed about her new job, irritated from being cooped up in the car with the restless kids, and cranky from the desert heat.

Amazingly, Gavin's spirits remained high. He'd fought Hannah on the move at first, but once he'd realized she could not be convinced, he'd done his best to help her make the necessary preparations. They faced many logistical challenges along the way. It was a move, after all, and moves were always a pain, especially for people with three kids and little money. Each time a new wrinkle would arise, Gavin would meet it cheerfully. Almost too cheerfully. Hannah was grateful he was in such a good mood, but she was also a little

suspicious of his good spirits. It was as if each new problem was
further proof he had been right all along, and they never should
have left Sacramento in the first place.

In the end it didn't matter; she was grateful for his support even
if on the inside he was giving her a secret "I told you so."

They had planned to make the trip in one day, but by the time they'd
reached Salt Lake City at eleven o'clock the previous night, Hannah
had been more than ready to throw in the towel. So the family had
broken out the credit card and holed up in a La Quinta Inn for the
night. After eating a questionable continental breakfast the next
morning, they continued their journey. Now they had finally arrived.

"Is *this* our new town?" Sage asked. She'd asked the same question
at each town they'd passed throughout the nearly eight-hundred-mile
drive. Fortunately they hadn't passed through many towns in the
boonies of Nevada and Utah.

"No!" Quinn answered with big-sisterly wisdom. "We'd never live
in a town like *this*. It's so . . .." She trailed off as she searched for
the right word.

Hannah looked out the window, but as the landscape of her family's
new town passed by, she too was lost for words. Off to the left, a huge
Confederate flag hung limp above a vast collection of ramshackle
trailer homes. A bony hound dog ran across a bare-dirt lawn to bark
at them, a strangely mournful "hoo hoo hoooo!"

On their right was a low, brick church designed in some pseudo-
modern, blasé 1960s architectural style, and to Hannah it didn't look
very well maintained. A crowd of people stood in front of it, the
women wearing dresses almost as brightly colored as the makeup

on their faces, the men clad in ugly polyester suits. Perhaps most strangely of all, everyone in the crowd seemed to be smoking a cigarette. There were so many smokers, Hannah thought—or maybe imagined—she could see a cloud of smog hanging over them like the stink that emanated from Pig-Pen in the Peanuts cartoons. The sign in the yard read, God the Avenger Baptist Church, and a special message spelled out in changeable letters beneath it: Do not practice homosexuality . . . .It is a detestable sin.—Leviticus 18:22.

Hannah gave Gavin a panicked look, but her concern seemed only to amuse him, and he gave her a playful grin and grabbed her thigh suggestively.

Just when she felt sure she'd seen all she could bear, they passed through the downtown area. "This doesn't seem so bad," Hannah said hopefully. The storefronts looked a little rundown, with more empty shops than she liked to see, but the town exuded quaintness and charm—or at least the potential for charm with a little paint and some entrepreneurial spirit on the part of the townsfolk.

"Look!" Quinn said, and the whole family looked off to the right. A celebration of some kind was happening in the park. Loudspeakers had been set up, and a fat old man with a wide-brimmed cowboy hat spoke quickly into a microphone as a band played country music furiously behind him. Townsfolk in hats and cowboy boots danced together, moving from one partner to the next.

"God, look at those outfits. What are they doing?" Hannah asked.

"Don't you mean *what is them folks doin'*?" Gavin asked playfully.

Hannah glared at him.

"It's a square dance, honey," he said.

"How do you know?" she asked. He pointed, and Hannah followed the gesture to a banner strung between two trees on one corner of the park. It read: Hickory Bluff Square Dance and Pig Cook.

"Pig cook?" Hannah said, wrinkling her nose.

"There!" Quinn gasped, and she pointed.

A complete pig carcass sat in a slow roaster, its skin scorched red, pink, and black. Hannah's gaze scanned from its feet to its intact snout, its closed eyes, its slack mouth, and its lolling, charred tongue.

"That used to be a pig?" Quinn demanded.

Sage screamed, which made Beau cry, which made Quinn shout at them both to hush up.

Hannah looked at Gavin and caught him chuckling.

"Hey, you're the one who wanted to move here," he said. "Welcome to Hickory Bluff."

• • •

Hannah spent the rest of the drive trying to look on the bright side. The mountains were beautiful. The sky was a vivid, pristine blue. The air smelled fresh.

Despite her attempt to think happy thoughts, she was still a little terrified as they turned onto the street where they would be living. They had rented a house sight unseen from a realtor Tara had referred them to and had seen quite a few pictures of the place. Still, after the disappointment the rest of the town had been, Hannah braced herself for the worst.

She was pleasantly surprised, then, when they pulled into the driveway of a bland-looking, sea-foam green bungalow. The place was small. Hannah preferred the term "modest," but she had to be real with herself: it was small, and it was all they could afford. But the lawn looked well maintained, and from the exterior at least, the house seemed to be in good repair despite the ugly paint job. It was on a normal street in an average middle-class neighborhood, and the mostly ranch-style houses that surrounded them, while not ostentatious, seemed to show some pride of ownership—all, that is, except one.

The house directly on their left was a major eyesore. Grayish paint flecked from its aluminum siding. The shutters that were not missing slouched from the window frames. The roof, too, seemed to slink downward as if to escape the embarrassment of crowning such an ill-maintained home. The lawn was mangy and brown, and two identical, filthy, cherub-like toddlers clad only in diapers squatted in a patch of bare dirt in the center of it, digging a pair of plastic shovels into the ground as if playing in a sandbox. Dirty toys, discarded power tools, and a broken aluminum ladder littered the yard. An out-of-season Christmas manger scene with a tipped-over Mary sat in one corner next to a broken-down old Buick.

Hannah took in the whole scene before discovering the lawn's most prominent ornament. In the center of the walkway, a woman lay in a lawn chair, clad in an impossibly tiny hot-pink bikini. The string that went around her neck had been untied, and the scant triangles of fabric they were designed to hold up had been pulled down to the lowest point Hannah thought was probably permissible by law, until her two areolas were peeked up from their tops like a couple of rising suns. The woman was slick and glistening with oil, and the reddish bronze of her skin was about ten shades darker than her bleach-blonde hair. A pair of cheap-looking, dangly earrings hung from her ears, and she wore a pair of stiletto heels. Hannah tried but found it impossible to keep from staring at her. A little pair of tanning goggles covered the woman's eyes, but even so, Hannah got the feeling she was aware of their presence too.

By then Quinn, Sage, and Gavin had all piled out of the car.

"Can we go see the backyard?" Quinn asked.

"Sure. Just don't wreck the place before we get moved into it," Gavin said before Hannah could respond, and the girls stampeded around the side of the house, leaving their brother asleep in his car seat.

"Be careful," Hannah called after them, envisioning a backyard full of broken glass and protruding nails. But they were already gone.

Hannah wandered a few steps up the driveway, taking in the house.

"Well, it doesn't look bad, does it?" she said.

"It looks fine," Gavin agreed. "Do you want to do a walk-through or just start moving in?"

Their conversation was interrupted by the sound of a pair of bare feet slapping up the sidewalk toward them. It was one of the tanning neighbor's toddlers. He—or she, Hannah couldn't tell—scampered right up to Hannah and held up a scoopful of dirt in a yellow plastic shovel, grinning.

"Hi. What have you got there? A shovel?" Hannah asked.

"Fuck," the toddler said.

Hannah tried to exchange a glance with Gavin, but he was looking at the child's mother; he couldn't seem to stop looking at her either.

Apparently realizing that Hannah hadn't understood the first comment, the child repeated his—or her—word: "Fuck. Fuck, fuck, fuck, fuck-fuck," the toddler said, then dumped the dirt onto his—or her—own feet and laughed delightedly.

"Vic. Git back here *now*!" the tanning woman bellowed without moving, screaming so loudly that Hannah jumped. She was amazed that a person could summon such ferocity and volume without even moving or opening her eyes. The toddler immediately turned and sprinted back to the desolate patch of earth where the other twin still played.

Hannah shook her head in wonder at the scene she'd just witnessed, but had no time to stand around and be amazed; they had a lot to do.

"All right," she said. "I'll take Beau in and do the walk-through. Why don't you start unloading. Gavin?"

Gavin, who had once more been caught staring at the neighbor, winced as Hannah slapped him on the arm.

"Sorry, she's just so . . .." He groped for words.

"Redneck? Sad? Begging for us to call child protective services?" Hannah supplied.

"I was going to say oily," Gavin said, giving Hannah a much-needed laugh.

• • •

A few hours later, Gavin had the trailer unloaded, the kids had the backyard explored, and Hannah was making progress on getting the kitchen properly cleaned when they heard a knock on the door. Hannah and Gavin both reached the door at the same time and answered it together. There, standing on the stoop, was their tanning-queen neighbor. She held a plastic bowl containing what looked to Hannah like a red jellyfish. Next to her stood a man in a V-neck T-shirt that looked as if it had formerly been white. He wasn't terribly overweight, but despite his average size, he had a strangely large stomach and a double chin. Large, dark bags under his eyes gave him the look of a mournful basset hound.

"Welcome to our 'hood,'" the woman said with a big, infomercial smile. Her voice was high and girlish, a sound diametrically opposed to the satanic bellow she'd issued to her child from the lawn chair a few hours earlier. She wore more clothing than she'd had on before, although not by much. Her T-shirt was tied to expose her midriff and was see-through enough that Hannah could still make out the pink swimsuit top beneath it. The cutoff shorts she wore were so short they barely covered her bikini bottoms.

"This is for you," the neighbor said.

"Thank you," Hannah replied, taking the bowl. Its contents quivered as she took it, reinforcing the disquieting idea that it was a jellyfish. Did they have jellyfish in Utah? Hannah didn't think so, but she thought it might be wise to Google it before she tried to eat whatever was in the bowl.

"It's Jell-O salad," the neighbor said, ending Hannah's speculation and beginning another one. How could Jell-O be a salad? The two seemed pretty much like opposites; one was healthy, the other was all sugar. It was baffling but no more baffling than everything else Hannah had seen in Hickory Bluff so far.

"I'm Nellie, and this is my husband, Daryl," the neighbor lady said. Her husband said nothing but gave a little nod of affirmation. "We have some kids too, so if yours want to come over and play with ours, that's okay by us. The more the merrier, right, Daryl? We love our play dates."

Daryl did not respond but gazed at Hannah with his sad hound-dog eyes.

"I'm Hannah, and this is my husband, Gavin," Hannah said.

"Nice to meet you," Gavin said, shaking Daryl's hand and then Nellie's.

A moment passed. Hannah glanced suspiciously down at the contents of the bowl. She'd had a momentary premonition that it was crawling up toward her.

"Well, we've gotta be getting back to the roost," Nellie said. "Just wanted to welcome you. Let us know if you need anything. Don't be afraid, we don't bite—much!" She giggled. "Ta ta!"

Nellie retreated from the porch, pulling Daryl along with her by the arm.

Hannah shut the door and instinctively locked it.

"Well, that's one problem solved," she said.

"What?" Gavin asked.

"Dinner," Hannah said. And she shook the Jell-O concoction in his face until, laughing, he was forced to retreat from the room.

# Chapter 6

With all the chaos of moving into a new home, Hannah didn't get to the grocery store until quite late. She passed the place twice before realizing she'd arrived at what her iPhone claimed was the only grocery store in town.

Back in California she'd preferred to shop at Whole Foods or Trader Joe's, although Ralph's Supermarket would do in a pinch. Hickory Bluff's grocery store, she realized immediately, was no Whole Foods. This place was called General Buck's, and it was set in a big, red, converted dairy barn complete with a silo attached. When she first pulled into the parking lot, she was confused. Until she spotted a family pushing a grocery cart out to their car, she had begun to imagine she'd stumbled upon a feed and grain store, and—God forbid—there was no store that sold human food in the whole village.

She felt some relief, then, when she walked into the barn and found it had been converted into a fairly normal grocery store with a typical produce section in the front, a deli counter off to the left, and a row of aisles along the back. Never mind that the place still held a whiff or two of scents left behind by the building's previous residents; she was starving, and she was glad the town had a grocery store at all. She thought it miraculous how fast a person's standards could change as she lugged a bag of oranges into the cart.

In her haze of weariness and growing hunger, she was most of the way through the frozen-food aisle before she got around to studying any of her fellow shoppers. The first one she noticed was a man with a bushy, walrus moustache and a cowboy hat. He knelt in front of a low shelf and was energetically sifting through bricklike bags of frozen spinach, examining them one by one as if one might be far superior to the others. The first thing Hannah noticed was his strange behavior; the second was the pistol holstered on his hip. She repressed a gasp then instantly chided herself for being so reactionary. It was probably from watching too much news lately, she thought. All those mass shootings. Obviously the explanation here was simple.

"You're a police officer?" she asked in the friendliest tone she could muster as she opened the glass door next to him and took out a bag of frozen corn.

The man's wild eyes stared up at her through a pair of thick-lensed aviator glasses. "No," he said a little peevishly. "Why?"

Hannah shook her head. "No reason," she replied in a mousy squeak of a voice then turned and put the corn in the cart. As calmly as possible, she pushed it down the aisle, around the corner, and back toward the front of the store, her pace increasing with each step.

By the time she'd reached the front of the barn—or store, or whatever it was—her heart was pounding.

She looked around for someone to report the man to, but the only employee in sight was the cashier, a skinny, doe-eyed teenager with flat bangs and long, crimped hair, the likes of which Hannah hadn't seen since the '80s. The girl was having a spirited conversation with the woman she was checking out. Hannah tried to find a place to butt in, but she couldn't; their conversation was seamless, like a suit of armor without any chinks, and she literally was unable to get a word in. In fact, she realized after a moment, neither woman gave the other a chance to finish a sentence.

"Isn't her new baby such a—?"

"Adorable. I told her to name her Jackie after her grandma, but—"

"I just can't imagine having a kid at her age, but God bless her—"

"Prettiest cheeks. I just want to squeeze 'em, and—"

"Shame that Sean left her, but he never was any good—"

"Hey, weren't those bananas on sale, hon? I thought I had a coupon—"

On and on the conversation went. Hannah was so intrigued by their obliviousness of one another—and of her, and of the several other patrons who waited docilely in line—that she soon gave up being afraid of the weirdo in the frozen foods aisle. If he opened fire, she'd run. In the meantime she got in the back of the line with her cart and prayed she would make it home before the ice cream melted.

Directly in front of her in line stood a woman with a young daughter. The mother was heavyset, with hair that looked as if the lower half of it had been dipped in bleach, and she stood flipping through a *National Enquirer*. The little girl was unfortunate enough to look like her mother. She also resembled D-list reality TV star Honey Boo Boo, closely enough to make Hannah do a double take. The girl was overweight; it must have taken some feat of engineering Hannah couldn't quite imagine to jam the poor girl into the cart's child seat. Every five seconds or so, the little girl would take in a big breath, causing her belly to poke out the bottom of her stained pink T-shirt (which had the word *princess* written on it in glittery letters) and expelled a deep, juicy-sounding burp.

"Momma, listen," the little girl would say, and she'd belch again even louder. The mother continued to ignore her. Each time the cycle repeated, the little girl increased in volume, so by the time the mother finally put her *Enquirer* down (having read the whole thing, Hannah guessed), the girl bellowed and burped so forcefully that Hannah was sure she would vomit at any moment. The whole sight was so disgusting, Hannah had to avert her eyes to avoid becoming nauseated. To distract herself, she decided to count the number of people in the store wearing coarse, brown Carhartt farmer's coats. She counted five. Six if she wanted to count a pair of Carhartt overalls.

Finally the belcher's heaping stack of groceries was dwindling on the conveyer belt, and Hannah went to start unloading her stuff. She reached into her cart and grabbed a milk jug and a soup can, but when she turned back, she found that someone had stepped in front of her in line. It was one of the Carhartt-coat guys.

She felt her face getting red with anger. A little bit of local color was one thing, but this store was starting to seem like a madhouse.

"Excuse me. Sir. Excuse me," she said to the back of the broad-shouldered, ponytailed mass in front of her. When the cutter finally turned, however, she was stunned to find it wasn't a man at all; it was a tall woman. She had on cowboy boots, dirty blue jeans, and a tattered flannel shirt. Her hair was reddish but about half gray. Her skin was rugged, lined, and leathery like a cowboy's, and her eyes were as gray as a wolf's. Hannah took her in at a glance, and her eyes traced down to notice one more thing: a six-shooter on her hip.

The woman stared at her implacably for a moment then turned away and tossed something onto the belt with a ponderous thunk. It was a pack of Marlboro reds.

*The Marlboro Woman!* Hannah exclaimed silently. The nickname hadn't taken any thought at all; it was as undeniable as gravity. The Marlboro Woman had just cut her in line. *This is too much! Wait until Gavin hears about this place.*

If she were still living in California—close to Hollywood, the mecca of all things contrived—she would have been sure she was the subject of some goofy candid-camera show. But no, she thought. This was real. More than real: it was now her life.

And if she were going to continue shopping here, she needed to do something about it.

"Excuse me, is there a manager here I can talk to?" she asked the cashier when the Marlboro Woman had left. The teen gave Hannah a strange look then called over the intercom for a manager. By the time the cart was loaded, no one had shown up, but the cashier pointed toward a counter made up to look like a small horse corral near the store's exit.

"Manager's right there. Have a buckin' good day," the girl said flatly and turned to the next customer.

Hannah pushed the heavy cart over to the customer-service corral, where a small, round-faced man with a pair of mutton-chop sideburns and a stained greengrocer's apron stood smiling at her.

"Well there, how can I be of service to you, little lady?" he asked.

"Well, I barely know where to begin," Hannah said. "First of all, someone cut in front of me in line."

The manager was already nodding. "Brenda," he said. "Yep. She does that. She doesn't wait."

He said it not with a tone of apology but as a man agreeing with an obvious fact, as if Hannah had said, "It looks like rain," and he'd said, "Sure does."

She decided to change tack. "Not only did she cut in front of me, she also had a gun. So did this guy in the frozen-food aisle."

The man was already smiling and nodding again, and Hannah really wished he would stop. "Yep, yep," he agreed and pointed to a sign on the wall behind him.

General Buck's: Your Local Gun-Friendly Grocer, it read. Next to it was a plaque bearing the National Rifle Association's logo. Hannah was still gaping at these artifacts when the manager came around the counter and approached her.

"What do you pack?" he asked.

"What?" she replied.

He reached to his side, where California grocers usually had pricing guns hanging, and pulled out a shiny revolver. "Ruger GP100. She's a classic," he said, brandishing the gun. "What do you pack?"

She felt an icy smile rise to her face. "Have a nice day," she said and wheeled her cart past the manager and out of the store.

Out of the thousands of panicked thoughts that crossed her mind as she loaded the groceries into the car, only two stood out. The first was: *I should really have gotten more than one bottle of wine.* The second was: *What on God's green earth have I gotten myself into?*

• • •

Hannah arrived home to find Gavin and the kids had settled into the living room. Someone had found and opened one of the boxes of toys, which were now strewn like a layer of storm debris across the entire floor. Gavin had set up the TV on the floor in one corner of the room, and a Disney moving was playing on it. Her husband sat on the couch with a laptop across his legs, sipping a beer.

Hannah was forced to take in all this information in only a glance because the bunches of heavy, plastic grocery bags she held felt like they were about to rip off her fingers.

"Hey, you got the TV set up," she said, trying to sound cheerful instead of how she felt—ragged, exhausted, and more than a little disturbed by her experience at the grocery store.

"And the Wi-Fi. I've been busy," Gavin said without looking up from the computer.

"Hi, Mommy!" Sage said and fiercely tackled one of Hannah's legs. Of course Beau then had to tackle the other one, and Quinn swooped in last, swallowing her other siblings in a group-hug sandwich.

"Hi, sweeties!" Hannah greeted the kids with a smile, but as their hugs grew more spirited, the scrum threatened to trip her and send her sprawling to the carpet.

"Love you all tons, but Mommy's got groceries," Hannah said, shaking herself free and fighting her way toward the kitchen while Sage and Beau continued to cling to her, sucking her downward like quicksand.

"Gavin, will you help me unload?" she asked on the way back through.

"Uh-huh," he said without moving.

Ten minutes later Hannah had the groceries unloaded and put away. She also had a frozen lasagna heating up in the oven. Her tasks done for the moment, she went into the living room to tell Gavin about her nightmarish shopping trip. He still sat right where she'd left him, lounging on the couch amid towers of unopened boxes, surfing the Internet.

"What are you looking up, the meaning of life?" Hannah asked.

"Huh?" Gavin asked, finally looking up.

"I said you look pretty focused. What are you doing, looking for jobs?"

"Oh. Yeah," Gavin said and rubbed his eyes, looking like the paragon of a man who'd spent hours diligently job hunting online. Hannah felt bad she'd been annoyed with him for not helping unload the groceries.

"You're not going to believe my trip to the store," she said, and she told him the details of her shopping experience.

Gavin whistled when she was finished.

"Wow. Sounds kind of like Mayberry on crystal meth."

"With guns," Hannah reminded him. "Lots of guns."

He nodded. The expression on his face didn't exactly say "I told you so" like it had before. Now he just looked distracted.

"I'm going to hit the commode. When's dinner?" he asked, rising.

"Thirty minutes. Will you help me chop veggies for a salad?" she asked, but he'd already disappeared down the hallway. A second later she heard the bathroom door shut. The kids were all engrossed in the movie, and, for a rare moment, Hannah found herself unoccupied. She could unpack boxes, of course, but if she got into that now she'd be up all night. Instead she picked up Gavin's computer. Maybe she could help him with his job search, she thought. Pick out a few promising posts from Career Builder, maybe, or track down the local newspaper's want ads online.

What she found in the browser window, however, was not a job-search site. It was a site listing area golf courses. She felt her good mood souring to anger.

She had been patient with Gavin back in California; she knew how tough the job market was, and she knew golf was an important outlet for him. But if he thought he was going to mess around here playing golf all day instead of finding a job, like he'd done back in Sacramento, he was sorely mistaken.

In her anger she clicked on the icon to bring up the browser's search history. Just when was the last time he'd done any job hunting anyway? she wondered.

What she found made her jaw literally drop. It was not a list golf searches, as she'd been expecting, or a list of basketball blogs or sports chat rooms or anything else she might have imagined. The whole history, from top to bottom, was filled with porn.

Judging from the page names, every type of pornography imaginable was represented. There was MILF porn, lesbian porn, and midget porn. There was ass porn, barely legal porn, German *scheisse* porn, and bestiality. There were black girls, white girls, Asian girls, Latina girls, girls next door, squirters, screamers, dominatrixes, and submissives. From the titles, Hannah could hardly imagine what some of the sites must have contained; others she understood perfectly, and their titles gave her way too many mental pictures. One thing was true across the board: the letters XXX came up as often as "www" did.

"Were you saying something to me?"

Hannah was torn from her thoughts by Gavin's voice; he stood in the doorway. In a panic she closed the browser window and banged the computer shut.

"Uh, salads?" she said.

Gavin shrugged. "Sure, why not?"

"I'll make it," she said, pushing the computer off her lap like it was something contaminated, and rising quickly.

"You want some help?" he asked.

"No," Hannah said quietly as she hurried past him. "You had a long day. Just rest and watch the kids."

The truth was, she didn't know what to say to him or how to feel, and she preferred to have a moment by herself to sort out her feelings. Alone in the kitchen, she leaned on the counter, trying to calm the twisting feeling in her stomach and the chaotic swirl of thoughts in her mind. So Gavin liked porn. Lots of guys did—maybe all of them, for all Hannah knew. There were worse things than that.

The sick feeling she was experiencing now was probably a classic overreaction, nothing more. She'd wake up tomorrow and laugh at herself for being concerned.

He was just watching movies. She'd watched plenty of movies in her day and could list a half dozen movie stars she thought were incredibly sexy. Was what Gavin was doing really any worse? And even if she did have reason to be upset, there was no time to get into a big discussion about it now, with a whole house to unpack and with her new job starting tomorrow.

Talking herself down in this way, Hannah managed to calm down enough to get dinner on the table, and she acted cheerful the whole rest of the night. By bedtime she was so exhausted, Gavin's twisted online activity barely even entered her mind—but the sick feeling in her stomach never quite went away.

# Chapter 7

At six o'clock on Monday morning, Hannah nearly sprang out of bed. Something inside her seemed to have been galvanized while she slept, and she woke to face the day with a feeling of fierce determination. Maybe their family was in a tough situation. Maybe Gavin wasn't cut out to be the breadwinner of the family. That was okay—Hannah was. She'd put her own career aspirations on hold when she'd become a mother. Now the work ethic, intelligence, and capability she knew she possessed would be released.

As she drove to work, the resplendent dawn painted the surrounding mountains with its gorgeous, vivid hues. She felt electrified with the certainty that she was capable of great things and that nothing in the world could stop her from achieving those great things, especially now, when all her family's needs rested on her shoulders. It was an incredible feeling. She felt closer to God in that moment than she had in many, many years.

The energy of the moment propelled her all the way up to the door that matched the address Tara had texted her: 601 Linden Avenue, Apartment C. She knocked three times, and at last the door opened, revealing a middle-aged woman wearing a stained scrub top and gray sweatpants. She had a cigarette in one hand and a TV remote in the other, and Hannah could hear some terrible talk show blaring in the background: the paternity of some poor woman's father was about to be revealed for whatever audience was pathetic enough to be watching at eight in the morning.

"Yeah?" the woman said and took a drag on her cigarette.

"I'm Hannah Martin. Tara said this is where I'm supposed to report for work. Are you Rachel?" Hannah asked tentatively, thinking she'd obviously knocked on the wrong door.

The woman's eyes got big, and she seemed to choke on her cigarette smoke. "Oh, oh, Hannah. So pleased to meet you. Please, come in."

The door opened wider, and Hannah followed the woman into the apartment. The place smelled strange, like a mildly nauseating mixture of old cooking and sweaty underwear. As Hannah watched, the woman—Rachel, she guessed—charged around the small apartment. She hurriedly stubbed her cigarette out on a saucer, gathered some dirty dishes off the coffee table, and jerked curtains wide open, revealing a rather dingy sliding glass door and a view of the stuccoed wall of the next building a few dozen feet away.

But Rachel wasn't alone. Two men sat on the couch, watching the TV. One of them was big—especially around the middle. He was shaped like a Russian nesting doll, and he wore a bike helmet covered with stickers, the most prominent of which was a rainbow that arched across the front from one of his eyes to the other like a great multicolored unibrow. The man sitting on the couch next to him was much smaller and had the pleasant yet distinctive features of a person with Down syndrome. Both men smiled at Hannah but made no move to greet her.

All the while Rachel was rushing around and talking. "I swear, I thought Tara said you'd be starting tomorrow or I'd have cleaned up the place. Don't want to give you the wrong impression, especially since you're the boss's friend! Normally this place is as tidy as can be." Plates in hand, Rachel now scurried across to the kitchen, opened up the dishwasher, and dumped the plates in—cigarette and all.

"Tara hates it when I smoke. Please don't tell her," Rachel pleaded, fanning the residual smoke from the air with her hand. "I try to quit, I do, but—it's an addiction, you know? Nicotine."

The two men on the couch suddenly laughed at something on the TV. The big one clapped his hands.

Hannah shook her head. She felt like she'd wandered into the Twilight Zone. "I'm sorry, I guess I'm just really confused here. I talked with Tara only briefly, but I thought this was supposed to be some kind of a home for special kids."

Hannah wasn't quite sure what she'd had in mind. Her phone conversation with Tara had been spent mostly talking about old times. Hannah had been so grateful for the job offer, she hadn't asked many questions, and Tara's tone had been breezy and confident. "You'll love the job. You'll be great at it!" she'd said, and Hannah had believed her. The e-mail Tara was going to send, which was supposed to contain more details, had never come. On the way here, Hannah had imagined her new place of employment would be something like a cross between Hogwarts and Yale, some ivy-walled, red-bricked bastion of gifted teens.

"Yep," Rachel said. "These are two of our special guys right here. In the helmet there is Ralph, and his little friend is Sebastian. John is still sleeping, but we should be waking him up soon."

Hannah blinked, finally beginning to understand. "Special... . ." she murmured. "Special *needs*. But . . . I don't understand. I was supposed to get an e-mail... .. .."

"Yeah, I sent you an e-mail a few days ago," Rachel said.

"I never got it!" Hannah exclaimed.

Rachel took a wadded-up piece of paper out of her pocket. With the other hand, she fished out her lighter and lit another cigarette. She squinted at the paper.

"Hannah dot Martin at G-nail dot com?" she asked.

Hannah rolled her eyes mightily. "Mail! G-mail dot com! Who ever heard of *G-nail*?" It sounded like one of the websites her husband apparently frequented, she thought, but was in no mood to make a joke. Suddenly it felt like her whole world was in chaos.

Rachel shrugged and glanced at her watch. "Well, I better skedaddle. I gotta visit my husband at the prison. You all have fun, all right? You have any questions about anything, just ask John. He's got the routine down pat."

Rachel headed to the door, pulling on her coat, but Hannah latched on to the back of it, detaining her.

"Wait. You can't leave me like this. I have no idea how to care for these people," she said in an intense whisper. "I haven't been trained. I'm not certified. I'm not qualified. I don't even know why that man over there is wearing a helmet."

Rachel gave Hannah a pitying look. "It's so he don't hit his head," she explained patiently.

From somewhere behind Hannah came what seemed to be—although it surely couldn't have been—the rumbling sound of a powerful, juicy fart.

"Oop. Sounds like Ralph made a doody. Extra diapers are in the bathroom," Rachel said, inching toward the doorway. Hannah grasped her coat even more tightly.

"Are you honestly telling me that man is wearing a diaper, and you expect me to change it?" she said to Rachel.

"You can do whatever you want, dearie," Rachel said serenely. "But that's the job. And if you think you can sit around all day with the smell of Ralph's dirty britches, you got a tougher nose than me."

With that she yanked her coat free of Hannah's grasp and escaped out the door.

Hannah hurried after her and stood in the doorway, watching Rachel stride away across the parking lot. She wanted to say something more, to beg or shout or threaten—anything that would bring Rachel back—but she already knew it was too late. Rachel had handed the torch to Hannah, and nothing in the world would make her come back.

With a deep sigh, Hannah steeled her nerves and turned back to the room. The reek of feces was enough to turn her stomach, and she suddenly felt so angry and overwhelmed she could barely hold back her tears.

On the couch, however, Ralph and Sebastian both giggled wildly.

• • •

That night Hannah went home after work and sat down at the kitchen table. She could hear Gavin and the kids out in the backyard, but she made no move to join them. More correctly, she didn't feel as if she could move—that was how utterly physically and emotionally exhausted she felt.

An e-mail came in on her phone, and she opened it and began to read. It was the detailed explanation of the job that Rachel was supposed to send Hannah before she'd started.

Hannah had spent half the day trying to convince Ralph to let her change his diaper, and when he'd finally let her she'd sort of wished he hadn't—that was how nasty it was. According to the e-mailed handbook, this was to be a normal part of her duties along with feeding the three men, bathing them, teaching them, and taking them on biweekly field trips. The job was nothing at all like what Hannah had imagined, and she wasn't sure who she was angriest at: Tara for failing to explain everything, Rachel for sending the e-mail to the wrong address, or herself for taking a new job out of desperation and moving her family hundreds of miles without bothering to read the fine print.

But what could they do now? The lease on the new house had been signed. The old house was on the market, and their realtor already had an offer on it. The savings were gone, and the credit cards wouldn't hold out for long. She had no choice but to make the job work somehow; the problem was she wasn't sure she could manage it.

Her bleak thoughts were interrupted by the sound of the sliding door opening, and the girls charged in and piled onto Hannah's lap, with Beau a few toddling steps behind.

"Mommy's home!" Sage trumpeted.

"Congratulations on the new job, Mom! We're proud of you," Quinn said with her trademark maturity.

"Rad-lay-sin," Beau said, which Hannah took to be Beau-speak for *congratulations*.

"Thanks for working hard, Mommy! We missed you!" Sage said and gave Hannah a big squeeze.

Gavin had come in too. He stood near the sliding doors, smiling.

"So, how's the new gig?" he asked brightly.

Hannah stroked Beau's hair and took a long, slow breath before replying. "I think it's going to be fine," she said finally. She couldn't bring herself to tell them the truth, not after a greeting like that. The funny thing was, in that moment she almost believed it would somehow all work out all right.

# Chapter 8

The next day, when Hannah arrived at the apartment for work, she found that Rachel was already gone. A note written on yellow, lined paper was attached to the door, and Hannah took it down and read it, squinting at Rachel's nearly illegible handwriting. She'd written that a field drip was scheduled for later that day. Hannah was to take the guys to the 12:15 showing of the latest Disney film at the local AMC. The tickets had already been purchased, and if Hannah kept her receipts she'd be reimbursed for the cost of any snacks plus whatever mileage she racked up on her car during the drive.

"Well, how generous," Hannah grumbled. Cash was tight enough without her having to spend money on her job and then wait to be reimbursed. But there were no boxes on the little note to check yes or no, so she guessed it was an order and not a request. A key was taped to the front of the letter. The words next to it read: "So you can let yourself in if I'm not here," with a smiley face next to it. Hannah wondered how often Rachel took it upon herself to cut out early and made a mental note to discuss her rather suspect coworker with Tara next time they talked.

After pulling the key free of the note, she entered the apartment to the sound of wild laughter. Ralph and Sebastian were both jumping on the couch and giggling—Sebastian in his underwear and Ralph in his massive diaper. From the bedroom came a voice she guessed must have belonged to John:

"Shhh, I'm sleeping. Guys, shhh, I'm sleeping. Guys, quiet. I'm asleep."

Already she knew it would be a long day.

During the car ride, Hannah was relieved the guys were well behaved. Randy got rowdy and started shouting out the window once, but Hannah said his name in her sternest mom voice, and instantly he piped down and remained quiet until they arrived at the theater.

On the way across the parking lot, the three men walked in a tight cluster, almost touching one another. Clearly someone had taught them to stay together in public, and they'd taken the order seriously. They approached the concession counter solemnly, and after some careful thought placed their orders. Ralph got a small popcorn and a king-size Kit Kat bar. Sebastian got a bag of Reese's Pieces. John's order was a little harder to make out. He was severely autistic and had a hard time communicating with people; usually he wouldn't even look at them.

Finally, after some gesturing, grunting, and head shaking, and a twenty-questions-like interrogation by Hannah and the acne-faced teenager behind the counter, they determined John wanted a large popcorn with extra butter. The look of supreme delight on his face when he received it confirmed it had indeed been exactly what he wanted, and Hannah felt a great sense of accomplishment at having deciphered his order.

As they all walked away from the counter, Ralph muttered: "Uh-oh, popcorn" under his breath.

"What, Ralph?" Hannah asked. "What's wrong?"

"John loves popcorn," Ralph said.

"Well, now he has some. That's good, right?" she asked.

Ralph looked skeptical. "John loves popcorn . . . *too much.*"

They'd gone only a few more steps before Hannah found out what Ralph was talking about. John threw a popcorn kernel up in the air and tried to catch it in his mouth. When it bounced off his face and dropped to the floor, he laughed delightedly. The next one he threw up hit him in the eye, and he laughed harder.

"John, stop," Hannah said.

John threw up another kernel. This one bounced off his upper lip.

"Uh-oh," Ralph said again, and he exchanged a look with Sebastian.

This time John took a whole handful of popcorn and hurled it into the air. As it rained down around him, he squealed with joy. Hannah reached out to pull the popcorn tub away from him, but he was too quick for her. He lunged out of her grasp, hurling another handful of popcorn into the air and cackling happily.

"John, stop. No more. Stop," she said, but the more she pursued him, the quicker and more elusive he became. She chased him in a circle around the two other men as, all the while, he tossed popcorn into the air like confetti at a ticker tape parade.

"Yay!" Sebastian exclaimed, basking in the deluge.

John was now squealing shrilly. It seemed the joy of the popcorn had been heightened by a rush of adrenaline from being chased, and he raced off down the hallway with Hannah in hot pursuit. The few midday moviegoers—elderly people and a couple of young mothers—watched in wide-eyed confusion as they passed. John no longer bothered to toss his popcorn by the handful. Now he simply jerked the whole bucket up and down, causing a cloud of greasy kernels to pelt Hannah across the eyes and face as she struggled to catch up to the amazingly speedy John. He screamed now with excitement and giddy panic, barreling toward a door marked Emergency Exit.

Hannah could just imagine the disaster that would ensue if he pushed those doors open and set off a fire alarm. The whole theater would probably have to be evacuated. The fear of that added em-barrassment gave her the final burst of speed she needed to catch John. She managed to grasp the back of his hooded sweatshirt and pulled it steadily backward, as if reining in a galloping horse. Strangely enough, John responded in much the way a well-trained horse would have—slowing to a jog then a walk, then a halt before finally stopping to turn his mischievous and rather sheepish gaze back toward Hannah, or toward her feet, which was the closest John ever came to making eye contact.

"Popcorn," he said happily, holding up the empty container for Hannah to examine.

"Yep," Hannah said wearily as she fought to catch her breath. "That's right, John. Popcorn." Only when she said it, it came out sounding more like a curse word.

• • •

The next morning Rachel was actually at work when Hannah arrived, but she breezed out the door so fast the two women barely exchanged a word.

"Food in the fridge. Outing to the mall today. It's on the calendar," Rachel said as she jammed her arms into her jacket sleeves, brushed past Hannah, and took off out the door.

Hannah found the calendar hanging on the fridge and saw that indeed, the words Outing: Fairview Mall had been scrawled on it in mint-green, sparkly ink. A quick search on her phone told her the mall was more than forty minutes away—way up near Provo.

She was starting to warm up to the guys. Each had his own quirks and charms, and they were sweet, but after yesterday's popcorn eruption she didn't think she had the strength to take them out in public again, much less on a journey that would require almost an hour in the car.

She'd called Tara the night before, hoping to get some pointers about how to succeed in her new role (and to discuss the grossly incompetent Rachel), but Tara hadn't picked up, so Hannah had left a voice mail. She tried her again now, and once again got her voice mail.

She looked at Sebastian and Ralph, who both sat on the couch patiently watching cartoons. She sighed. Hannah had never been a person to shy away from a challenge or to give up, especially when her family relied on her. Besides, she was the mother of three children; surely she could manage to take three grown men to the mall. All she had to do was make sure John didn't get his hands on popcorn or any other confetti-like substance.

Hannah's confidence wavered a little when it took her almost four hours to get the guys up, dressed, and fed. Once they were in the car, though, things went a little more smoothly. As they rolled out of town, Hannah scanned the radio, finally settling on an oldies station. Ralph was delighted and began to sing along (albeit completely off pitch and with an average lyrical accuracy of maybe one correct word per song). John, however, hated the music. He clapped his hands over his ears and screamed until Hannah shut off the radio. They rode the rest of the way in silence, entertained only by the scenic grandeur of Utah.

Finally they reached the mall. Hannah managed to get the car parked and the men herded into the mall without incident. Her companions drew a few strange looks from shoppers, especially from one blonde teenybopper who almost dropped her Macy's bags as she gaped at Ralph's helmet. But one fierce look from Hannah was enough to send the girl fleeing into Victoria's Secret, and her little horde of cheerleader buddies went along with her.

The day went on, and the trip was going fine. Better than fine—it was going great. Using some of the petty cash Rachel had left for her, Hannah treated the guys to big, soft pretzels. (John hardly ate any of his, but he didn't throw it either, which Hannah counted as a victory.) Then she bought them all zesty, orange-flavored drinks from Orange Julius. They were getting ready to head back to the car when Sebastian stopped in his tracks in the middle of the walkway, pointed, and squealed. Hannah followed his gesture to a pet shop. In the window several adorable, fluff-ball kittens were playing together, leaping, wrestling, preening, and napping in a display filled with play ropes, carpeted tunnels, and ledges.

"Kitties, right, Sebastian? Do you like kitties? You like animals?" Hannah asked.

Sebastian grinned so hard his eyes crinkled shut.

"You want to go look at them, guys? Come on, we can go, but not for too long. We have to be back in time for me to make you some dinner."

The crew shuffled into the pet store. John stopped near the entrance transfixed, gazing into a bin filled with pet toys—colored balls, knotted ropes, and squeaky stuffed animals. Ralph and Sebastian, however, made a beeline for the left side of the store, where a glass display wall separated the customers from cages filled with all sorts of pets: puppies, hamsters, rats, lizards, birds, and even to Hannah's mild disgust, snakes and tarantulas.

Hannah followed them, but she made sure to keep one eye on John in case he decided the toys in the bin would make amusing projectiles. He didn't try to pick them up, however. He simply stood perfectly still and stared at them as if they were the most interesting objects in the world.

Meanwhile, Sebastian walked up and down in front of the glass wall, taking in all the animals. Ralph seemed to be fixated on a fluffy white Maltese puppy.

"Aww!" he said, looking to Hannah then back to the puppy. "Aww!"

A young store clerk with pixied pink hair and a nose ring approached. "Cute, isn't he? That's Bozo. You want to see him?"

Before Hannah could protest, the girl disappeared to the other side of the partition and emerged a moment later with the squirming puppy in her hands. Ralph clapped in excitement as the store clerk handed the dog over to him.

"I'm not sure if—" Hannah began, but it was too late. The girl had already handed the dog over, and Hannah soon realized her fears were for nothing. Ralph was incredibly gentle with the puppy, cradling it like a baby and snuggling his face against its soft fur.

Hannah abruptly wheeled around at the sound of a squeak. Behind her, John had started to dig through the vat of dog toys and was now pulling them out and dropping them on the ground as if looking for something.

"John, you can't do that. Those aren't ours, okay? Stop!" Hannah said. She took the squeaky, stuffed chipmunk John held and put it back in the bin, then gently grabbed John's wrist when he tried to take it out again. "John, no. We can't do that," she said.

John gazed at his feet, looking neither disappointed about being scolded nor happy about the mess he'd made. With a sigh, Hannah apologized to the clerk and started putting the scattered toys back in the bin.

"Oh, it's fine," the girl said. She seemed to be having fun watching Ralph love on the little dog. When Hannah had most of the toys put away, she suddenly stopped and looked around. John was right next to her. Ralph was over by the wall with his new friend. Where was Sebastian?

At that moment the first clue swooped out at her. It was a brightly colored parrot, and it had appeared from the same door marked Employees Only that the clerk had left open when she had gone to get Ralph his puppy. Hannah watched with mounting horror as a parade of animals skittered out the open doorway.

A battalion of puppies came first, barking and falling all over one another. Then came a lizard and a swiftly slithering snake. The latter wriggled right past the clerk's feet, and she screamed and ran away to the safety of the checkout area. A knot of kittens and hamsters made their way out the door while a flurry of birds shot past above them, twittering and cawing. There were loping ferrets, scurrying gerbils, and scrambling white rats. Hannah dashed forward to try to herd them back through the doorway, but when she saw a tarantula creeping toward her, she retreated as quickly as she'd advanced, taking shelter behind John's bin of toys.

If the guys were concerned about the menagerie flooding toward them, they didn't show it. John had picked up a ball with a jingle bell inside it and was jiggling it in rapt fascination. Ralph exchanged licks with the puppy.

Hannah looked up and saw a familiar face behind the glass wall. As she watched, Sebastian opened a cage with a young beagle in it, grabbed the dog around its middle, and pulled it out. Hannah almost tripped on it as she ran through the door and into the employees-only area.

"Sebastian, stop!" she shouted.

For the first time, a look of remorse crossed the man's normally happy face, and she instantly regretted the harshness in her voice.

"What are you doing?" she continued more gently, approaching Sebastian and taking his hand. "You can't do that. You can't just let the animals go free. You have to pay for them."

"They can go free," Sebastian disagreed.

"No, they can't, Sebastian. I'm sorry. Come on."

She led him out of the back area and into the main store. The scene was utter pandemonium. Shoppers screamed and ran. One employee dashed around with a net, trying to catch birds, while another had a potbellied pig under one arm and tried to drag a pair of frightened kittens out from under a display rack. The girl with the pink hair seemed to have recovered her courage and was gathering up gerbils and hamsters, depositing them into a big pocket in the front of her Pet Universe apron. Outside the store, scores of passing shoppers had stopped to gawk at the disaster. Several had their phones out and took pictures and videos, which Hannah was sure would end up on YouTube in a matter of minutes. Amid all the chaos, John and Ralph seemed like the only two sane people in the world. They stood quietly, watching Hannah and Sebastian as they approached.

"Come on, Ralph. Put the dog down. Thank you. Let's go," Hannah said. She grabbed John's hand, gripped Sebastian's tighter, and headed out of the store with Ralph a step behind.

"They can go free," Sebastian said again once they'd made their way through the crowd of spectators. No one answered, so he said it again louder. "They can go free."

"You set them free all right," Hannah said. "But I don't think they're going to let us visit that pet store again."

Ralph found that funny, and he started to laugh. Sebastian laughed too, a big, bright, full-voiced guffaw. Even John smiled. By the time they made it to the parking lot, Hannah was laughing right along with them—but she was crying a little bit too.

• • •

On the way home from work, Hannah stopped at the grocery store.

After the day's events, she felt ragged, weary, and so discouraged that she wasn't sure she could bear to go back to work and face it all the next day. What if she simply couldn't hack it at this new job? . How could she explain to Gavin that she'd dragged the whole family hundreds of miles to a completely foreign town only to fail at the job she'd gone there to accept? And what would happen to them if her income disappeared? Had Gavin even bothered to start his job search in Hickory Bluff? Somehow she doubted it.

Given her current emotional state, she would have preferred to go home, wrap up in her coziest robe, climb into bed with some cookie dough ice cream, and then drift off to sleep—or maybe take a hot bubble bath. But they were out of milk, and with three growing kids and a husband who loved his breakfast cereal, she had no alternative but to stop and pick it up. In a way she was grateful to have a moment alone, away from the bedlam of the guys' apartment and the pleasant chaos of her home. She was actually beginning to calm down a bit by the time she reached the checkout counter—until she saw a familiar, looming figure lurch toward her clutching a bottle of bourbon, a package of Oreos, and a pack of cigarettes. Hannah recognized the stony face and the coarse brown coat immediately. It was her nemesis: the Marlboro Woman.

*No way. She's not going to*—but Hannah didn't even get a chance to finish the thought. Without so much as a moment's hesitation, the big woman stepped directly in front of her, taking her place in line.

Hannah was a patient woman, but this was going too far.

"Excuse me," she said, and tapped the woman on the shoulder. Slowly she turned around, leveling her cold, hard eyes at Hannah. Under their glare she felt her resolve waver. "You, um. You stepped right in front of me."

The woman continued to look at her. "I know," she said in a gravelly voice, then turned to face forward again, leaving Hannah to stew in her outrage. She didn't have the strength to fight this woman. Not the physical strength nor the emotional strength. She felt tears welling in her eyes, but she fought them back. She might let this woman bully her way to the front of the line, but she'd be damned if she gave her the satisfaction of seeing her cry. By the time she made it up to the cash register, her eyes were dry.

"Hi. How's your day going?" the cashier said when Hannah stepped up.

"Fine," Hannah said. It was perhaps the most flagrant lie she'd ever told.

• • •

She was in a haze of exhaustion by the time she got home. The beautiful, wide western sky was fading into the deep purple of twilight, so she barely even saw the little toddler who ran in front of her car as she pulled into her driveway. She gasped and slammed on the brakes so hard her seat belt snapped taut across her chest, and for a second she was terrified she'd hit the child. But it emerged a moment later, giggling and pants-less, holding a filthy Cabbage Patch Kid in its pudgy arms.

"Hey, you need to be careful, sweetie," Hannah said out the car window. The child only giggled and ran back into the neighbor's yard. Hannah cursed under her breath and carefully pulled into the driveway. Nellie the neighbor had been bent over, scratching at the parched earth of a flowerbed with a little rake, wearing a tennis skirt that barely covered her butt cheeks. She turned around now, took the cigarette out of her mouth, and adjusted the huge, too-glamorous sunglasses that covered half her face.

"Don't pay them kids any mind, hon. They run around like chickens with their heads cut off all day, but they have the sense to get out of the way of cars," Nellie said.

"Well, that was a pretty close call," Hannah replied. "Maybe you should have a talk with them, or—"

But Nellie had already gone back to working on her so-called garden—or displaying her ass to the neighborhood, which Hannah suspected was the more likely motivation for her behavior. As Hannah watched, she chugged the last of a beer from a can she'd set in the dirt next to her, dropped her cigarette into the can, shouted something unintelligible to one of the two toddlers, then tossed the beer can into a bucket that sat on the porch overflowing with what Hannah hoped were at least a month's worth of empties.

"Oh my God, we have to get out of here. This town is insane," Hannah whispered.

• • •

Hannah forced a smile onto her face as she stepped into the house, ready to confront the happy onslaught of her family. Sure enough, within seconds Beau was wrapped around her legs, Sage skipped in circles around her, and Quinn talked a mile a minute, describing how she and her new friend Joselyn had braided each other's hair at school. Gavin arrived a moment later, pausing long enough to kiss Hannah and take the grocery bags out of her hands before asking what was for dinner.

She managed to keep it together long enough to cook a stir-fry and have a nice sit-down meal. Afterward Gavin sweetly volunteered to clean up the kitchen while she put the kids to bed. When she returned to the living room, she found him in front of the TV watching some shoot-'em-up movie starring Bruce Willis.

"Hey babe—" Gavin greeted her, but she nosedived before he could finish, flopping onto the couch on top of him.

"Whoa, what's going on?" Gavin asked as she nuzzled into him.

He put his arms around her, and she felt the day's tension loosen its grip on her clenched muscles. She launched into a monologue:

"I just don't know, Gavin. I don't know if I can do this. I feel like a terrible person. I uprooted our family, I dragged you all over here. But Tara told me it was a good job, and I trusted her. How was I supposed to know that Ralph wears a diaper or that John loves the way popcorn looks when it's exploding through the air? How was I supposed to know that Sebastian is a crazy animal-rights crusader who hates seeing creatures in cages? And now I'm cleaning up shit and picking up popcorn and dressing grown men, not to mention dodging runaway gerbils and kittens and snakes and tarantulas. And Rachel is no help whatsoever. Every time I see her, she's like a runner in the middle of a marathon: 'Hello, good-bye, just passing through. Oh, you don't know what the hell you're doing? Just check the calendar on the fridge, hon. See ya!'"

Gavin tried to interject, but Hannah continued.

"And then the Marlboro Woman freaking cut in line on me again today! Do you believe that? I'm not taking it anymore, Gavin. I don't care if she has fifty guns. I don't care if she's a female Billy the Kid—next time she tries to step in front of me in that grocery line, I swear to God she's going to be sorry."

Gavin looked at her wide eyed. "So let me get this straight. Are you telling me you changed a grown man's diaper?" he asked.

"It's not just that," Hannah said desperately, balling up his shirt in her fists and tugging on it. "It's—it's—"

"It's everything," Gavin finished for her, and he gently pulled her close again, wrapping her up in a big, tight hug. "I get it, babe. It's a hard job, and you're not used to working. You're used to being home with the kids, and I'm sure you miss them like crazy. Our finances are tight, and, to top it all off, we're in a new place, with all the stresses of moving and settling into a new town. But don't worry. Pretty soon I'll be working, and you can go back to being at home with the kids."

She sat up a little and looked at him. "You're right. This is a hard job, and I'm not entirely sure I can hack it. But . . . I do like working, Gavin. Even if—I mean *when*—you find a job, I might want to have some kind of career. How would you feel about that?"

She braced herself for a negative response and was relieved when he smiled. "I would feel like you've always been a smart, capable woman who happens to be stubborn as hell. If you decide to work, you're going to be amazing at it, and I wouldn't try to stop you even if I could."

She felt a blush rising in her cheeks and an uncontrollable grin taking over her lips. Gavin didn't compliment her much, but that only made it all the more meaningful when he did.

"Thanks for understanding. I really do like working, but this job . . .." She shook her head. "How's your job hunt coming? Any leads yet?"

He shrugged but didn't answer. Hannah didn't figure that was a very good sign. But did it mean he hadn't found anything yet or, as she feared, that he hadn't been looking at all?

"Come on," Gavin said suddenly, and he scooped her up in his powerful arms and rose to his feet.

"Where are we going?" she asked. In her voice she heard some of the giddiness she'd felt when she and Gavin had first started dating. He was so tall and strong, and when he picked her up it was always a major turn-on. He pressed his lips to her ear.

"I'm taking you into our bedroom," he whispered. "And then I'm going to undress you, and I'm going to get out the massage oil, and I'm going to give you the best massage of your life. And then I'm going to—"

She laughed and shushed him with a kiss as he carried her across the threshold of their darkened room.

They made love that night. It was an exquisite release that Hannah hadn't realized she needed so desperately until it happened. After it was over, she lay awake in the darkness for a long time, staring at the outdated ceiling fan hanging above the bed, catching her breath and enjoying the moment. Gavin was asleep in seconds, and she lay next to him, feeling his breathing, feeling his warmth against her body.

It had been a rough couple of months, she thought, but they were making it through. They had three wonderful kids. They had each other. And because of the job she now had, they were able to pay their bills and survive. Gavin's faith in her gave her renewed faith in herself, and suddenly she knew that as long as her family was counting on her, she could—and would—handle anything. She would endure whatever was necessary to make sure they were okay, even if it meant finding a way to deal with Ralph, Sebastian, and John. Before she drifted off, she watched Gavin sleep for a few moments, reflecting on how wonderful their night had been.

She was completely unaware that it was the last time they would make love for a long, long time.

# Chapter 9

◇◇◇◇◇◇◇◇

Three months later, Hannah arrived home from yet another brutal, twelve-hour shift at work. Before she'd left, she'd gotten a text from Gavin saying Quinn had some big science project due the next morning, and she needed poster board, glue sticks, glitter, and a whole list of other supplies. So, as exhausted as she was, Hannah had stopped off at the drugstore to get the art stuff.

Now she stood in her driveway, wrangling the shopping bags out of the car and fantasizing about how good it would feel to flop down on the couch and finally put her aching feet up. That was when it happened.

"Hey, Hannah."

The voice was so close it was almost in her ear, and it nearly made her scream and drop the bags she was holding. Instead she wheeled around and found one of her two favorite neighbors leering at her. Hannah had come up with nicknames for her colorful neighbors over last few months. This was Creepy Daryl, the husband of Naked Nellie.

One of Creepy Daryl's creepiest traits was that he was a close talker. This problem was compounded by the fact that he had extremely bad halitosis. But even though Daryl stood only three inches from her, and she could feel his hot, stinky breath wafting on her cheeks, that was not destined to be the worst part of their interaction that evening. It was the words he said next that momentarily made her world stop spinning.

"You know your husband is banging my wife," Daryl said casually.

For a moment Hannah stared at him dumbly as his words sunk in. Then she felt her face redden. She tried to figure out what to feel—anger, disbelief, outrage—but she couldn't seem to settle on one thought or emotion. She felt like she was standing in the middle of a raging river, her thoughts pieces of driftwood rushing past too quickly for her to grasp.

She thought of slapping Daryl for saying such a horrible thing about her husband, but her hands were full of bags. She thought about laughing in his face. But, God forbid, what if it were true? She thought about thanking him for telling her—but what if it were a lie? Of course, it had to be a lie!

Daryl was talking again. "You seem like a smart woman, so I'm sure you figured it out awhile ago. I just thought maybe we should have us a chitchat in case you need me to, you know, talk to your divorce lawyer or something. I'm a pretty good shoulder to cry on, too, if you need one."

*Awhile ago?* Was he saying this had been going on for a while? *Divorce? Shoulder to cry on?*

"I'm sorry. Nellie is a real mess. A certified nymphomaniacal sex addict, that's what she is. Cheated on me the first week we were married. I paid for her to get a shrink, two hundred bucks a week of my hard-earned money. Then I found out she was boning him for like three and a half years. No shit. You can't make this stuff up."

Daryl looked at her, his ugly bBassett-hound eyes filled with pathos. "You need a hug?" he offered, opening his arms and swooping in on her. She shrugged him off and finally found her voice.

"Excuse me," she said forcefully. "I don't know what you think you know about your wife, but my husband would not cheat on me. All right? You're mistaken."

She turned on her heel and walked up toward the house.

"You don't believe me?" Daryl said. Something in the way he said it made Hannah hesitate, and she turned back to look at him.

"Stand between our two houses tonight at nine fifteen," Daryl said solemnly. "You'll see."

• • •

Daryl's accusation gnawed at Hannah all evening: through dinner, while she emptied the dishwasher, as the family watched TV together. She didn't say anything, though. As the hours wore on, she grew more and more confident in the conviction that neighbor Daryl was as insane as he looked. The idea that Gavin would cheat on her was ludicrous, much less that he'd do it with a trailer-trash harlot like Naked Nellie. The painful tension in Hannah's gut was just starting to relax when Gavin abruptly got up from the couch.

"Well, I'm going to hit the shower," he said. He gave Hannah a peck on the lips and then headed for the bathroom.

When she glanced over at the clock, she felt like a brick had hit her in the chest. The time was 9:12.

"All right, time for bed," she announced quickly, clapping her hands together. Beau was already in bed, but after persistent begging, the two girls had been allowed to stay up a little longer.

"Aww! But the show isn't over!" Sage protested.

"Yeah, Mom. Please?" Quinn rejoined.

"You heard me. Bed," Hannah said. "If you're both in your PJs, teeth brushed, and in bed in the next three minutes, I'll make you Mickey Mouse pancakes for breakfast tomorrow, okay? Now go!"

The girls tore off like a couple of dragsters,. and. sure enough, by nine fifteen they were both snug in bed. When all else failed, Mickey Mouse pancakes always did the trick.

Hannah turned on their night light, gave them each a kiss, and then walked out of the room, leaving the door open a crack, just the way they liked it. On her way to the front door, she glanced at her watch. Nine sixteen.

*This really is crazy. What am I doing?* Hannah asked herself as she stepped out into the night.

She felt sick with nerves, but she forced herself to move calmly and steadily as she walked around the side of the house and crouched in the big clump of bushes that marked the dividing line between the two properties. From there she could see the bathroom window where Gavin was inside, taking a shower. The blinds were down, and light shone out through their horizontal slats. The neighbors had a window directly opposite Hannah and Gavin's. Most of the houses in their little subdivision were different versions of the same floor plan, and Hannah imagined that the neighbor's house was probably a mirror image of her own—therefore the window she was looking at was probably a bathroom window too. A light was on in there as well, but the view inside was concealed behind a pair of frilly pink curtains.

Hannah waited for a moment, looking from one window to the other, and then smiled, laughing at herself. Of course she had nothing to worry about! Creepy Daryl didn't know what he was talking about. How had Hannah believed him even for a second? Boy, was Gavin going to make fun of her when she told him about this.

She was just getting ready to extricate herself from the bushes when the light changed, and she looked over to see the neighbor's curtains opening. There, framed in the window, was Nellie. She had on even more makeup than usual and was wearing a silky, hot-pink robe tied so loosely it barely covered her ample breasts, and it stopped just inches below her baby-making parts. Hannah watched as she stood in the window as if waiting for something.

Hannah's eyes snapped to her own bathroom window just as the blinds rose. The sight she saw through that window made her clap a hand over her mouth.

Gavin stood behind the glass completely naked.

Hannah's eyes flicked to the other window again, in time to see Nellie dance, moving her hips suggestively as she slowly untied the robe and let it fall. Her hands then began moving up and down her body. Hannah felt a twinge of nausea. She blinked furiously at her rising tears. With some effort she forced herself to look back at her own bathroom window. Gavin had one hand against the glass. With his other hand, he stroked himself.

"Oh God!" Hannah heard herself say. Unable to watch any more, she thrashed backward out of the bushes and stumbled back to the porch. She stood there for several minutes grasping the rusting wrought-iron railing for support while she caught her breath and gulped back her tears.

The images she'd just seen sizzled through her brain like acid. No matter where she looked, she could still see it: Nellie dropping her robe, Gavin with his hand pressed to the window, licking his lips luridly. A kaleidoscope of emotions played over her then, from sadness to pain, from disbelief to disgust to rage.

Finally she managed to calm herself. The whirling emotions settled and solidified into a fury that sat in the pit of her stomach like a cold, hard stone. Eyes dry, heartbeat steady, and hands barely shaking, Hannah released her grip on the railing, stood up straight, brushed the leaves from her clothes, and strode back into her house.

● ● ●

Hannah stood in the hallway, staring at the closed bathroom door, wondering what to do next. When she heard the shower start up, she got her first burst of inspiration. She walked down the hall, opened the door to the water-heater closet, found the valve that controlled the hot water, and twisted it shut. Then she hurried back to the bathroom door. Seconds later she heard Gavin squeal then curse loudly. It was petty, but his suffering almost brought a smile to her face.

Moments later she heard the water shut off. She could imagine Gavin behind the door, fiercely drying himself off and grumbling about the faulty water heater. She waited patiently, and soon the door opened, revealing Gavin. He stood in front of the sink, wrapped in a towel, a toothbrush in his hand. He still had a little shampoo in his hair, and he looked annoyed.

"Hey, Hannah," he shouted, loud enough for her to hear him if she'd been in the living room. "Check the pilot on the water heater, would ya? The damned hot water is out."

"I know," Hannah said quietly.

Gavin glanced over and started when he noticed her there, standing quietly in the unlit hallway, watching him.

"Jesus, you scared me," he said, his mouth full of toothpaste. He went back to brushing his teeth and then paused. "Wait, what do you mean you know the water heater is broken? Did you try to fix it?"

"No," Hannah said. "I know because I shut it off."

Gavin quit brushing and glared at her, his eyebrows knitted together. Then he turned to the sink and spat.

Hannah felt the anger she'd been keeping in check rising within her like the first clouds of a rising monsoon. She started working the wedding ring off her finger.

"What the hell do you mean? You shut the water off on me?" Gavin said when his mouth was clear.

As soon as he looked at her, Hannah flung the wedding ring at him. It hit him right in the eye and bounced off, skittering across the linoleum floor and finally clinking down between the slats in the heating vent, gone.

"Ow! Fuck, Hannah!" Gavin exclaimed.

"Exactly, Gavin. Wow, you got it right on the first guess."

"Got what right?" Gavin howled, covering his eye with his hand.

"*Fuck.* That's the reason I'm mad at you. Because of who you fucked."

"I don't know what you're talking about," Gavin said.

"I'm talking about you naked with your junk in your hands, standing in the window for the whole world to see, while that diseased trailer-trash tramp next door puts on a show for you."

Gavin did not respond for a moment. He merely stood, his mouth slightly open, staring at Hannah with his one good eye. If she hadn't been so angry, it would have been almost comical, the sight of him with the remnants of shampoo in his hair, toothpaste drizzling down his chin, one hand over his eye, his mouth gaping in stunned bewilderment. Comical or maybe sad. But at that moment, Hannah felt neither sympathy for her husband nor amusement.

"You would destroy our marriage, break my trust, and put our children's happiness at stake—over *that*?" Hannah demanded. "Why? Tell my why, Gavin. Did you fall and hit your head? Are you on drugs? Is there some reason, or have you just lost your mind completely?"

Gavin had been slumping, but he stood up taller now. He took his hand away from his eye and blinked, then sniffed. The eye looked a bit red but didn't appear to be seriously injured.

He cleared his throat. "Yes, okay. You caught me. I've been sort of—playing around with Nellie. And yes, there is a reason for it. It's because of you."

Hannah gave him a stare that she was sure could melt an icicle. "Excuse me?"

"Well, what do you expect, Hannah?" Gavin said. "You're gone all the time. This damned job of yours—you work twelve-hour shifts, you get home, and you're exhausted. Then you're up late, reading up on all that junk—autism, retardation, whatever those guys you babysit have. There's no time for me, no time for the kids. I feel like I'm alone. I feel like I'm a single father. So I was acting like I was single. What do you expect?"

"What do I expect?" Hannah asked. She felt her voice rising but tried to quiet herself; the last thing she needed was to have the kids wake up in the middle of this. "I don't know, Gavin. Why don't you refer to our marriage vows if you'd like to know what I expect? Being faithful was one of them, I think. For richer or poorer. For better or worse. Yes, I have been working hard, but how else are we supposed to pay the bills? Who's going to pay for you to go golfing twice a week? And how's your job hunt coming, by the way?"

Gavin's face contorted with anger. "Hey, I used to work to support this family too, you know. I never complained when you stayed home. And—correct me if I'm wrong—I was never too tired to meet your sexual needs, was I?"

Hannah threw up her hands. "You're an animal. You're disgusting. I can't even look at you. So this is my fault? That's what you're saying?"

"No," Gavin hedged. "That's not what I'm saying. I'm just saying maybe you should take responsibility for your half of the problem here."

Hannah shook her head. Too angry to respond, she walked away. In the bedroom she tried to shut the door, but Gavin pushed his way in behind her.

"Baby, listen to me. I love you," he said.

"Go to hell, Gavin," Hannah replied, sitting down on the bed.

He knelt in front of her and grasped her hands. "No, I mean it. I love you. I want you. You're the only one I've ever wanted. I just . . . I've missed you. I've felt so lonely here all by myself."

"All by yourself? What about our three kids?"

"Baby," Gavin pleaded. "I'm a man, okay? Men are weak. Maybe you can run a house and have a job and cruise through life without any physical affection, but I can't. I just—can't."

"Then you shouldn't have made those marriage vows, Gavin," Hannah said. She pulled away from him and flopped down on the bed, then crawled up toward the pillows. All this time she'd managed to keep up her defenses, to stay angry, to fight back, but now the cracks in her armor started to show. Beneath the strong exterior, a howling chasm of pain was about to swallow her up. And the worst part about it, the thing that tortured her more than anything else, was the idea that maybe Gavin was right. Maybe it had been her fault that he'd gone astray. Maybe she wasn't there for him enough. Maybe she wasn't hot enough for him or sexy enough. Maybe she didn't do the right things. Maybe she was starting to get older, past her prime. After all, even her own father barely spoke to her. Maybe there truly was something wrong with her.

She buried her face in the pillow and sobbed. Gavin was still speaking, running his fingers through her hair, rubbing her back, apologizing, pleading, explaining, but his words were just noise to Hannah now, nothing but meaningless background music to the pain that felt like it was ripping her in two. A few times she tried to shake off Gavin's hands as he touched her shoulder. She shrugged him off when he tried to kiss her tear-soaked cheek.

Eventually she quit resisting and let him hold her, and when her sobbing finally ebbed away, she drifted off into the blackness of a dreamless sleep.

• • •

The next day, when Hannah got home from work, she found the house quiet and dark.

It had been a relatively smooth day at work. The guys seemed to sense there was something off with her, and they were a little quieter than usual, as if they were afraid to test her patience. When she took a break from the seemingly endless chores and tasks that comprised her workday to sit on the couch for a few minutes and watch TV with the guys, Sebastian sat down next to her and put his arm over her shoulder.

"My buddy!" he called her, his guileless eyes bright and his mouth smiling. Hannah had smiled too and wiped a tear of gratitude from her eye.

Even amid all the business her workday required, the thought of Gavin's betrayal was never far away. It was like a villain in a horror movie, always waiting to spring out at her—in the plot of a soap opera, in the sight of John's wrinkled button-down shirt so much

like one of Gavin's oxfords. It waited to startle her at the strangest
of moments, to cause the smile on her face to wither, and to make
her stomach twist into painful knots.

*Gavin cheated.*

*He betrayed me.*

*With Nellie.*

Through a mixture of distraction and denial, she'd managed to
get through her workday. When she reached her little home, she felt
even more exhausted than usual. It was hard enough to run around
all day caring for people, but to do so with such a heavy burden on
her shoulders was almost too much to bear. She paused for a moment
after she shut off her car, building up the mental strength required
be the strong, happy mother she wanted her kids to see when she
walked through the front door.

Except now that she was inside, the house seemed to be deserted.
She heard no laughter, no blaring TV; there weren't even any lights
on. Wait, now she saw something—a flickering, golden glow coming
from the kitchen. Setting her purse down on the hall table, she moved
cautiously toward the light.

"Hello?" she called.

"Hello."

She rounded the corner and stopped, stunned by what she saw.

The kitchen table glittered with silver. It was covered by a white
tablecloth and set with Gavin and Hannah's good wedding china.
A bottle of wine sat on ice in a bucket next to a vase full of roses.

Gavin stood near the kitchen island, wearing one of Hannah's
aprons. It had a green and pink floral pattern on it and was decidedly

too small for him. He had on a pair of oven mitts, too, and clutched a baking dish full of sizzling food. Hannah recognized it by the smell even before Gavin spoke.

"I made cannelloni, your favorite," he said. "There's also garlic bread, sautéed squash and onions, and wine. I didn't know what you'd want for dessert, so I got five different options—"

"Gavin," Hannah interrupted. "You didn't have to do this, okay? I mean, you shouldn't have done it. Where are the kids?"

"Across the street at Grandma Gem's," Gavin said.

Grandma Gem was a sweet old lady. She'd watched the kids once before, when Hannah and Gavin had spent a date night together a few months ago. She seemed like a kindhearted woman, and the kids adored her. Still, Hannah was not about to let Gavin off the hook.

"You can't just dump the kids off on Gem and expect to fix everything with a little Italian food, Gavin. What you did was . . . it was . . .."

She was getting worked up, but Gavin put a gentle hand on her shoulder. "Hannah. I'm sorry, okay? Truly, deeply, completely sorry. I'm not asking you to forgive me. I'm not asking you to forget about what I did. All I'm asking is that you sit down, eat some cannelloni, and have a glass of wine with me. Please?"

Hannah glared at him for a moment, but the rumbling in her stomach distracted her from her anger. She'd never known Gavin to cook before, but the food *did* smell good.

"All right," she said finally, "but only because I'm starving."

They ate together. The food really was amazing, and they were both so focused on eating that they didn't talk much. They were about halfway through their meals when Gavin cleared his throat.

"This isn't just an 'I'm sorry' meal, by the way," he said. "It's also a celebration."

Hannah looked at him. "What are we celebrating?"

Gavin grinned and raised his glass. "I got a new sales job. It pays almost as much as the one in Sacramento did, if you can believe it."

He clinked Hannah's wine glass with his.

"You know what that means," he said.

"What?"

"Hannah, it means you can quit your job. No more man-babysitting . . . man-sitting . . . whatever it is you call it. No more changing dude diapers. No more—"

"I get it," Hannah interrupted. The food and wine had put her in a slightly better mood, but she was getting angry again. "Do you think you can just get a job and that will make everything okay?"

"No," Gavin stammered. "I—"

"I like my job, Gavin," she said, then paused. The statement startled her. She didn't realize how much she'd grown to enjoy her new career until that moment. But now that Gavin was threatening to take it away, she felt defensive. "I like it," she continued, "and whether you're working or not, I'm going to keep it. You've proven I can't trust you, Gavin. I'm not going to rely on you like I used to anymore. I can't."

She expected him to throw a fit, but he didn't. Instead he surprised her by reaching out and taking her hand.

"I don't expect you to," he said gently. "I want to earn back your trust. What I did was wrong, I know that. And I will never, ever touch another woman again. All I ask is that you give me a chance to make it up to you, Hannah. If you do, I swear to God you will not be disappointed."

His beautiful blue eyes shone with emotion in the candlelight. His hand squeezed hers, and she could feel the strength in it; it was a feeling that had always made her feel strong too—and safe.

"All right," Hannah said at last. "One more chance. But if you ever—"

She didn't get to finish the sentence, because Gavin stopped her with a kiss.

# Chapter 10

◇◇◇◇◇◇◇◇◇

Ralph and Sebastian stared at Hannah with rapt fascination while John sat in a chair at the kitchen table, equally enthralled by a Rubik's Cube Hannah had gotten him.

"Sexy is always in style, and this season is no exception. Check out Jennifer's wispy, shimmering summer dress by Zuhair Murad paired with a sequined Judith Leiber clutch." Hannah turned the magazine around to show the men the picture. Sebastian's eyes got big, and he laughed happily. Ralph clapped.

A few weeks ago, Hannah had taken a small time out from her work to flip through a *People* magazine. Sebastian had sidled up next to her and urged her to read it to him. She'd tried to explain it was a celebrity gossip rag and not a real book, but he'd been insistent. When she had read it to him, he'd been delighted. Soon Ralph joined in. Now, reading *People* or *Cosmo* had somehow become an indispensable part of the guys' daily routine, and if she forgot to do it or tried to omit it, they always reminded her.

"Read me girl book!" Sebastian would say.

This one was a *Cosmo*. She had to skip all the sex articles, but the guys didn't know the difference.

"Ooh," Hannah said. "Here's Natalie Portman in Vera Wang." Before she got a chance to show off the picture, she heard a knock at the door.

The guys squealed in protest when Hannah set the magazine down and rose, but she told them they'd finish reading in a second, and they calmed down.

It was probably Rachel at the door—she was always forgetting her purse. Or maybe Tara was making a surprise visit. It was about time she did; in the months Hannah had been working for her, she'd seen Tara only once, when she breezed in to get Hannah to sign some tax documents.

But when Hannah opened the door, she found that her visitor was a man wearing a nicely tailored suit.

"Can I help you?" she asked.

"Hi, I'm Bryan. I'm here for Sebastian," the man said.

Hannah stared at him in blank confusion. She hadn't heard anything about this. "Okay. You're here to . . . ?"

"Oh, I'm sorry. I talked to a Rachel on the phone. I guess she didn't tell you I was coming. I'm Bryan LeVasseur, Sebastian's brother."

Hannah felt the tension drain from her body, and she smiled.

"I'm sorry. Please, come in," she said, opening the door wider. Before the visitor was even in the room, Sebastian squealed and ran over, clamping his brother in a bear hug that ended in a ring-around-the-rosy sort of dance. Sebastian's brother—Bryan—seemed just as happy to see Sebastian as Sebastian was to see him, and despite the fact that he wore a fancy suit, he didn't seem at all afraid to dance around and make a fool of himself if it would make his brother happy.

"What have you been up to, bro?" Bryan asked, clapping him on the shoulder.

"Read girl book," Sebastian said.

Bryan gave Hannah a sidelong glance. "You let them have girly books in here?" he asked slyly.

"Oh no," Hannah said, laughing. Then she explained about the magazine.

Bryan spent most of the day with the guys. Within minutes he'd shed his jacket and tie, and was soon up to his elbows in finger paint. He shared their lunch of macaroni and cheese and hot dogs. He helped John with a Lego project he was working on. When it was time, he even watched the guys' favorite show with them: *America's Funniest Home Videos.*

Sometimes Hannah was involved with their games; other times she went about her business, making food, cleaning up the kitchen, and vacuuming. All the while, however, she watched the brothers interact. It was incredible how well Bryan handled Sebastian and his friends.

When Hannah's work was done, she sat down in the La-Z-Boy by the couch. The guys were engrossed in the TV and didn't even notice her arrival—except Bryan.

"Listen, thanks so much for taking care of my brother," he said. "I have a law firm in Salt Lake City. It keeps me pretty busy, so I don't get down here as much as I'd like to, and I worry about Sebastian a lot. It really is a load off my mind to see he's being looked after by someone like you."

Hannah felt a swelling of pride at the compliment. She'd been watching Bryan all afternoon, but this was the first moment she really took him in. He wasn't as tall as Gavin and didn't have the same runway-model looks, but he was an attractive man. His hair was dark and stylish, his eyes big and brown, with eyelashes Hannah noticed even from three feet away. But more than looks, something intrinsic in him—his warmth, his kindness, a certain light in his eyes—made him not just handsome but magnetic.

He glanced at his watch then looked up at Hannah and smiled. "You know, I'm heading back to Salt Lake in a bit, but I was thinking of grabbing dinner. I don't suppose you'd like to join me?" he asked.

Hannah opened her mouth to reply, but for a moment the words caught in the back of her throat, and there was no sound. She felt herself blushing. Finally, she managed to say, "Thanks. I appreciate it, but—I mean, I would love to, except my husband will be expecting me."

Bryan winced, then laughed. "I'm so sorry," he said. "I would never dream of hitting on a married woman. It's just that you didn't have a ring."

Hannah glanced at the bare ring finger on her left hand. For a split second, she considered confessing that it had fallen down the heating grate after she'd bounced it off her cheating husband's face, but she decided against it.

"I—I lost my ring. Long story," Hannah said finally.

Bryan was on his feet. "I should really be going," he said politely.

"Mr. LeVasseur—"

"Bryan," he corrected.

"Bryan," Hannah said. "Please, I'm not mad—I see how good you are with Sebastian and how much he loves seeing you. I don't want you to be afraid that there'll be any weirdness between us if you come to visit again. I want you to come again. I mean, you're welcome anytime. For Sebastian. It won't be awkward, I swear."

Bryan smiled at Hannah's little outburst, and then he laughed. After a moment's hesitation, Hannah laughed too.

"Well, as long as it won't be awkward," Bryan said, giving Hannah a charming smile.

He said good-bye to the guys, gave Sebastian a big hug, and then headed to the door.

"It was nice meeting you," he said to Hannah, and gave her a businesslike handshake. Then he was gone.

Hannah closed the door behind him and then lingered a moment before turning back to the room. The guys had all gone back watching TV—even John, who had finally abandoned his Rubik's Cube.

It was good that Bryan LeVasseur was gone, Hannah told herself. Now they could get back to the day's routine. Plus it really would have been awkward to spend any more time with him after he'd asked her out like that. It was good that he'd left.

But without him the apartment already felt a little bit lonelier.

# Chapter 11
◇◇◇◇◇◇◇◇◇

The birth of Hannah's first child, Quinn, had been a grueling and harrowing process. The water had broken at three3:00 a.m. four weeks before her due date. Something went wrong when the doctors administered the epidural, and Hannah soon found herself vomiting profusely. After some minutes of head scratching, the doctors discovered she was losing spinal fluid. Hannah persevered, however, and after three and a half agonizing hours of pushing, Quinn finally came into the world. Little did Hannah know her trial was only beginning.

Once the tears, laughter, and videotaping were finished, and perfect baby Quinn had been bundled off to the nursery, Hannah tried to shift her weight in her bed and discovered her legs wouldn't move. Initially the nurse shrugged the problem off, assuring her that sensation would return. It didn't.

Two days later, after an exhaustive battery of tests, the specialists gave her grim news. Her femoral nerve had been damaged during the birth. They told her she would never walk again.

The prospect of losing her active lifestyle—not to mention trying to earn a living and care for a new baby while suffering from a disability—was terrifying. Still, Hannah was a fighter. Whatever she could do to regain function, she told the doctors, she would do it.

What followed was a regimen of intensive, excruciating physical therapy. At first Hannah could hardly stand up. Eventually she was able to move a bit but only with the aid of a walker. After five seemingly endless months, she was finally able to walk again, and soon her gait had returned to normal. The residual limp was so slight no one even knew it was there—except Hannah.

The ordeal was one of the hardest things she'd ever experienced, and the beginning of her time in Hickory Bluff reminded her of that painful, frightening process. But eventually, just as she'd conquered the complications of Quinn's birth, Hannah began to get a handle on life in Hickory Bluff.

It helped that Gavin was now working. His extra income took a lot of pressure and stress off Hannah, and he was always making thoughtful little gestures—like taking the kids out for weekend "daddy day" outings, bringing home presents, or taking her shopping—that were designed to make up for his disgusting affair with Naked Nellie. Hannah was still angry and hurt almost beyond belief, but she was so caught up in spending time with the kids, improving things at work, and the million other details of everyday life that she was surprised to find her anger fading little by little.

The hardest part of her life now was her work. She was sick of the misery and the struggle of it, but most of all she was upset because she felt like the guys she was working with could have happier lives if only she knew how to help them better.

So, late at night after the kids were asleep, and with Gavin snoring next to her, she would sit up and research their diagnoses on the Internet. She thought long and hard about the challenges each one of them faced and brainstormed things she could do to make things better for them.

The revolution began on a Wednesday, when Hannah showed up at work with a present under her arm. As usual, Rachel breezed past her as she came in the door, but she paused when she saw the gift.

"What's that? Is it one of their birthdays today? Tara usually e-mails me," she said. It was typical Rachel—she'd been working with the guys for the last three years, but she didn't know a single one of their birthdays by heart.

Hannah put her irritation aside. "Nope," she said. "This is just a gift for fun."

"Well, aren't you a sweetie," Rachel said with a tinge of fake sweetness that bordered on disdain. Then, as usual, she took off out the door at a full power walk.

Hannah turned to find the three men watching her eagerly.

"A present?" Ralph asked.

"It is. It's for Sebastian," Hannah said.

Sebastian squealed and clapped his hands, and all three men hurried to the table in the dining area. Hannah could almost hear Rachel's grating voice from some past birthday party, telling them, "No one's getting a present until everyone's sitting at the table." Whatever faults the guys might have had, they were always incredibly eager to please.

Hannah took the open seat and pushed the wrapped gift across the table toward Sebastian. His eyes shone with excitement, but he waited to tear into the paper until Hannah told him it was okay. Then he ripped it open with alacrity. As he stared at the box, however, his excitement dwindled to confusion. The box's contents were pictured, but. Sebastian didn't seem to know what to make of it.

"Here, let's look inside," Hannah said, and she tore the tape seal off the top of the box and pulled out two blocks of Styrofoam packing material—which Ralph immediately picked up and clacked noisily together.

The anticipation was almost too much for Sebastian, and he leaned forward in his chair, banging his hands on the table in agony, adding to the ruckus.

Hannah found the switch on the bottom as she pulled the gift out, and she turned it on as she set it on the table. It wagged its little silver tail and barked.

"I know how much you like animals, Sebastian. This is a robot dog just for you," Hannah said. The metallic-silver plastic dog scampered to the edge of the tabletop and barked playfully at Sebastian, who stood up, whooping and giggling in excitement.

"Do you like him?" Hannah asked.

"Yes, oh yes, yes!" Sebastian said, and he reached out one hand to pet his new companion's head tentatively.

"Why don't you take him over onto the carpet, and you can all play with him. Just be careful not to break him, okay? He can be hurt just like a real puppy." Hannah soon realized this was an unnecessary warning. Sebastian scooped up his dog as gently as a mother cradling her newborn baby, carried it into the living room, and carefully set it down in the middle of the rug while the other guys watched intently.

They spent the entire rest of the day playing with the dog. It had a special red ball that came with it, which it was somehow able to fetch, and the guys took turns throwing it. No matter how many times the dog brought it back, Sebastian and Ralph seemed as amazed as they had been the first time. John occasionally lost interest and went back to working on his Rubik's Cube, but he would check back in on the fun occasionally, especially if the robo-pup barked.

Hannah felt incredibly good, seeing the guys having so much fun and knowing that Sebastian's need for animal companionship was finally fulfilled. She didn't quite understand how much it meant to him until near the end of her shift.

Hannah had created and enforced a rule that dogs—even robot ones—were not allowed at the table, and Sebastian had to fight with all the willpower he possessed to keep from getting up from the dining table and running back into the living room, where his new friend waited. Every twenty seconds or so, he'd glance over at it with a look of such longing that Hannah found almost as touching as it was comical. Sebastian followed the rules, though, and refrained from going over and getting his pet until Hannah told him it was okay. When she did, he stood up and stampeded into the other room so fast he nearly tripped on his chair. He immediately snatched up the robo-dog, held it under his chin in a passionate embrace, and petted its head with one hand.

Ralph and John came over and sat down on the carpet nearby, almost as eager as Sebastian was to play with the new toy.

"So, you like your new dog, Sebastian?" Hannah asked.

He nodded so hard, he almost tipped himself over backward.

"What are you going to call your doggie?" she asked. "Does he have a name?"

Sebastian grinned up at her. "Hannah," he said.

•  •  •

The next day Hannah showed up bearing another gift. Sebastian was convinced it would be another dog for him (he assured her that this one, too, would be named Hannah), but she informed everyone that this gift was, in fact, for John.

Over the last few months, she'd learned that his love of dispersing things was not limited to popcorn and animal toys. Once Hannah had come out of the restroom to find the kitchen covered in an explosion of Cheetos. Another time the whole apartment was scattered with silverware. Then there was the worst John moment of all: the famous coffee grounds incident, which had forced Hannah to mop and vacuum for days.

After each of these episodes, John had seemed rather aloof about the whole situation. If she tried hard enough, she could wring a confession out of him, but that didn't mean it wasn't going to happen again the minute Hannah turned her back. She could see plainly that he didn't think there was anything at all wrong with what he'd done. Hannah tried various methods in an effort to avert the problem. She asked, begged, scolded, bribed, commanded, punished, and pinky swore. She even made him sign a contract—which he got ahold of the next day, tore up, and scattered so thoroughly that Hannah found little shredded bits of it on the top of the blades of the ceiling fan. It was then that she resorted to her last hope: she sat down with him and asked him outright.

"John, why do you scatter things?"

He seemed to think about this for a moment, then, in a rare moment of connection, he raised his eyes to hers. He opened his arms wide, puffed out his chest, and opened his hands, fingers splayed, as if trying to make himself as big as possible.

"To be everywhere," he said. "Be everywhere." There He spoke with a stirring urgency in his voice, a lucid desperation, but in the next instant it was gone. His arms clasped against his sides once more, his shoulders hunched, his gaze drifted to the floor, and he was cut off again. But Hannah didn't forget his wish.

Now, as he dug into his gift bag, she felt a smile creeping onto her face.

He looked a little perplexed as his hand emerged with his present. It was a bright-red plastic jar with a colorful label and a white lid.

John set it on the table and looked at the floor.

"Do you know what it is? Let me show you how to use it," Hannah said, and she carefully unscrewed the cap and pulled out the wand attached to the inside of the lid. It was made of plastic and had a small ring on the end. The ring was filled with the shimmering, quivering sheen of soapy liquid. She held it up in front of John's lips.

"Blow on it," she coaxed.

But he didn't. He stayed perfectly still, his eyes locked onto the linoleum at his feet.

Hannah brought the wand to her own lips and blew. A stream of delicate bubbles soared away on her breath, wafting through the room. Ralph and Sebastian both reacted with laughter and shouts of delight, and their loud response made John look up. When he saw the bubbles drifting around him, he gaped in wonder and excitement. He reached to snatch one from the air, but of course it disappeared the instant his fingers touched it, which further amazed him.

Hannah dipped the wand into the solution and blew another series of bubbles. They filled the air now, wafting throughout the room like lazy, round fairies.

"Me?" John asked.

Hannah dipped the wand again and handed it to him. "Just blow into it—not too hard," she said, and he did. Dozens of bubbles filled with his breath flickered to life and floated away. He blew again and again until the entire dining area was filled with the round, iridescent globes. At last John paused, out of breath, and took them all in. One moved toward his face, and he gently blew it across the table.

"Everywhere," he said in wonder. "Everywhere, everywhere, everywhere!"

• • •

Hannah's gift for Big Ralph, as she affectionately called him, wasn't as playful as her gifts for Sebastian and John, but it was definitely more urgently needed. At least it was needed by her.

Six or seven times a day, a smell would overtake the apartment. Sometimes Sebastian would notice first, and he'd squeal, point at Ralph, and then bury his head in a couch cushion. If John were the first to notice, he'd simply get up and leave the room no matter what he was doing. Once he caught the scent when he was helping Ralph load the dishwasher. He simply dropped the plate he was holding, letting it shatter on the floor, and ran away down the hall without a word.

When Hannah would get a whiff, her responses varied. Sometimes she groaned or sighed. Other times she'd just grit her teeth and say, "Okay, Ralph. Time for a diaper change"—once she'd managed to choke back the nausea.

Ralph's dirty diapers often weighed as much as a small bowling ball, and the smell was like that of a medium-size dead animal wearing a suit of limburger cheese on a balmy afternoon hayride at a pig farm. In a word, they were disgusting.

The diaper-changing task was by far the worst part of her day and became a sort of symbol of all the discontentment she felt with her life. Six to eight times a day, she was given a fragrant, highly unpleasant reminder of just where she stood in the pecking order of the universe, and on a few occasions it was depressing enough to make her lock herself in the bathroom for several minutes afterward and cry.

Just as she had with the other problems with her job, however, she soon decided to quit crying and complaining and instead face it head-on. While the guys were busy watching their afternoon TV, she'd be on her phone, busily researching gastric problems on the

Internet. She was pretty sure nobody should have been having as many bowel movements as Ralph was, and she reasoned he had to have an allergy or an ailment of some sort. Systematically she tried cutting things out of his diet—eggs, gluten, and finally the winner: dairy.

Hannah replaced the milk on Ralph's breakfast cereal with almond milk, quit putting cheese on his lunchtime sandwiches (which he never even noticed), and began using dairy-free alternatives for the guys' dinner. And voila: Ralph's diapers began filling much less frequently—and the smell got better too.

The result was that Hannah dreaded going to work much less. Ralph's life quality improved too, since he liked having his diaper changed only slightly more than Hannah liked changing it. But she wasn't satisfied yet.

Why couldn't Ralph use the toilet? Neither Rachel nor Tara seemed to know. When Ralph's mother had put him into their care, she'd explained he was never toilet trained and wore diapers. Changing his diapers had become one of the required care standards in his Compassionate Solutions file ten years ago, and that was how it had been ever since.

When was the last time Ralph's mother had tried to potty train him? Had she tried when he was a toddler and then simply given up? Had anyone tried to teach him since? No one seemed to know, so Hannah set out to try for herself.

That was why she now stood in the middle of the guys' apartment wearing a camouflage rain poncho, with a teddy bear in one hand and a bag full of Jolly Ranchers in the other.

"All right, Ralph. Let's try the potty again. I'll let you hold the teddy bear," Hannah said.

Ralph eyed her warily.

This was the third time today she'd tried to get him to use the potty. The first time he'd refused to sit on the toilet. It was hard to understand what he was saying, but she finally surmised he was afraid he'd fall into the commode and get flushed down. She'd tried to explain that the laws of physics simply wouldn't allow a six-foot-two, 290-pound man to disappear down a toilet drain, and at last he seemed to reluctantly believe her reluctantly.

The second time they'd tried, she'd managed to get him to drop his pants and sit on the toilet. As he gingerly eased his butt onto the seat, however, his elbow hit the flush lever. The sound of the water suddenly rushing out from beneath him made him panic. He sprang up to escape, but because both his legs were bound up by his dropped pants, he lost his balance. He ended up falling backward, with one hand jamming directly into the toilet bowl. He panicked even more and yanked the hand out as quickly as possible, trying desperately to shake the wetness from his fingers. The water was tinged blue from the 2000 Flushes automatic toilet bowl cleaner, leaving a smattering of blue polka dots on Hannah's favorite white top.

That was what had prompted her to go out to the car and grab Gavin's rain poncho.

With her protective gear in place, Hannah was ready to give it one more shot.

Ralph got up reluctantly from the couch and reached for the bag of Jolly Ranchers Hannah held.

"No, not yet. You can have one after you use the toilet, okay?"

Ralph pushed his bottom lip out in a pout that looked rather out of place on his big, stubble-covered face, but when Hannah took his hand and led him toward the bathroom, he didn't resist.

"Okay, pants down. You know how," Hannah said. Ralph stared at the toilet, then shook his head emphatically.

"Come on, it's not going to flush this time," Hannah urged, but Ralph only gave her a petulant frown and backed away. At that moment Sebastian appeared in the doorway.

"I have to go," he said, and pointed to the commode.

Hannah got an idea. "Will you let Ralph watch you? Show him it's safe? I'll give you a Jolly Rancher."

Sebastian seemed skeptical, but after staring at the Jolly Ranchers for a long moment, he finally nodded.

Hannah steered Ralph to a sitting position on the edge of the tub and instructed him to watch Sebastian. Then she retreated, stepping out into the hallway and closing the door part way to give Sebastian as much privacy as possible under the circumstances. Given the long series of grunts and farts that followed, Hannah once again reconsidered her line of work, but more than once, she found herself fighting to hold in a giggle.

Finally the sound of the toilet flushing announced that the task was finished. Hannah opened the door to find Ralph already pulling his pants down eagerly and plopping down on the toilet, an ardent grin on his face. Sebastian was scrubbing his hands at the sink—he was a diligent hand washer—and when he was finished, he expectantly extended one wet hand toward Hannah.

"A deal's a deal," Hannah said, and she deposited one green Jolly Rancher into his palm.

At the exact same moment, they heard the sound of a manful groan and a plop, followed by a stream of urine hitting the water.

Sebastian turned to Ralph and applauded. "Yah!" he shouted.

More clapping sounded from behind them, and Hannah turned to find John in the doorway. Ralph, still sitting on the toilet, beamed with pride. Not wanting her reluctance to clap to be mistaken for disapproval, Hannah clapped too. The three gave Ralph a much-deserved standing ovation for what seemed like quite a long time.

After a meticulous toilet-paper lesson and a vehement lecture about the necessity of hand washing, Hannah allowed the triumphant Ralph back into the living room. There, in the presence of his proud friends, she presented him with not one but three Jolly Ranchers: a purple one, a blue one, and a red one.

The only person on earth who could have been happier than Ralph at that moment was Hannah. Ralph's diaper era was over at last.

• • •

That night, on the way home from work, Hannah stopped off at the grocery store. Gavin was coming back from a long sales trip that evening, and she wanted to make sure he had all his favorite food stocked for the weekend. She was in a good mood, and not just because she was eager to get her "husband fix." Her triumphs at work had left her feeling empowered, and she felt an extra spring in her step as she made her way through the now-familiar aisles.

When the last item had been checked off her shopping list, she made her way to the front of the store and into the checkout line. As usual, the checkout girl was taking forever. And as usual, after a few moments, a familiar hulking figure approached. By then Hannah had decided the Marlboro Woman must have gotten out of work at the same time she did. Her nemesis gave Hannah a brief, dismissive glance with those cool, narrow cowboy eyes of hers, and—as usual—stepped in front of her in line.

But Hannah had something unusual planned. She grinned as her hand slunk into her purse, coming out with Quinn's bright red squirt gun, which she'd stashed in her purse that morning for this express purpose. The plastic weapon was heavy, sloshy, and moist to the touch—because it was loaded.

A housewife who stood nearby perusing the *People* magazines gave Hannah a horrified look as she leveled the squirt gun at her rival's head. Hannah paid her no mind, and instead cleared her throat and spoke in the kindest, gentlest voice she could muster.

"Excuse me, ma'am, but I believe you stepped in front of me in line."

The Marlboro Woman didn't turn around but responded with a flip of her hand over her shoulder, the nonverbal equivalent of, "Whatever. Buzz off."

"I warned you," Hannah said. She pulled the trigger, and she kept on pulling it.

She never would have thought such a stolid-looking woman would be capable of such a shrill scream; she sounded like a ten-year-old girl getting a purple nurple. As the cold water drizzled down the woman's neck and into the collar of her work coat, her shoulders contracted in a violent shrug. She swung around and looked at Hannah, a look of shock and confusion on her face.

Hannah, however, had no mercy. "No cuts," she said, and she pulled the trigger again, hitting the woman right between the eyes with a stream of water that spattered off her face, drizzled down her nose, and left her sputtering. With the next shot, she hit the cigarette pack in her hand, soaking it.

"No cuts!" Hannah repeated.

She heard the man behind her grumble: "She cut in front of me too one time."

The woman being rung up chimed in. "She's cut in front of me too. No cuts!"

"No cuts!" Hannah shouted in unison with the other woman. Soon the whole checkout line chanted loudly, "No cuts," and Hannah continued to spray her nemesis, squirting in time with her shouts.

The Goliath began backpedaling toward the door. She slipped on the wet floor and nearly fell but managed to right herself. The soggy cigarette pack fell from her hand as she careened off a magazine rack before finally turning and fleeing the store.

As soon as the Marlboro Woman was gone, the store patrons erupted with cheering and laughter. Hannah got quite a few pats on the back, and one older gentleman even complimented her on her shooting.

"You done the right thing, sugar," the checkout girl said when Hannah reached the cash register. "That woman was a no-good bully. I'm glad somebody finally taught her a lesson."

Hannah smiled modestly.

"Well, I wasn't trying to be a hero," she said. "I guess I'm just realizing you can't wait around for the world to start treating you right. You have to make it happen for yourself."

The checkout girl nodded slowly, taking in the profundity of Hannah's wisdom. "That's real good," she said. "You mind if I quote you on my Facebook wall?"

And the girl took her phone out then and there and updated her Facebook page while the rest of the store's patrons waited.

• • •

Before Hannah even reached the front door, Gavin had opened it for her, a bouquet of flowers in his hand. He greeted her with a kiss and then helped her bring in the groceries. Inside, Hannah found the kids all engrossed in productive activities. Quinn worked on her homework, Sage sat on the floor drawing in a sketchbook, and Beau lay on the couch, quietly playing an educational game on the iPad. The house was spotless, and the savory aroma of some sort of delicious food wafted through the air.

"Wow, Gavin. You've been busy. Is that dinner I smell?" she asked.

"It is, and it's just about ready."

"You've been driving all day! I was going to cook you dinner," she said, but Gavin shook his head.

"Too late. I beat you to it. Come on."

The food was as delicious as it smelled, and while they ate, the kids regaled them with stories from their lives. Quinn described a friend of hers who had tried to dye her own hair while her mom was in the other room and got hair dye all over the family's new carpet. She was now grounded. Sage told them about a boy in her class who talked only in the voice of some Japanese animation character with a name Hannah didn't think she could even pronounce. Apparently the voice was quite annoying, but no matter what anyone did—even the teachers—the boy's obnoxious impression persisted.

Beau contributed to the conversation by repeatedly lifting his fork in the air and declaring, "Mackychees! Mackychees!" WhichThat, of course, was how he referred to his favorite dish: macaroni and cheese.

Gavin went next. "I had a big hit. I hit the top sales tier, which means 5 -percent higher commissions across the board for the month. And I landed three new customers."

"That's awesome, honey! Nice work," Hannah said.

"What about you? How are things going at work?" Gavin asked.

Hannah told them about how she'd overcome the biggest challenges that Ralph, Sebastian, and John were facing, and then finished by relating her conquest of the mighty Marlboro Woman. Everyone thought it was hilarious—even Beau, who laughed so hard he almost choked on a piece of macaroni. Quinn offered to let her mom keep the squirt gun as a trophy to commemorate her victory (and because, she said with a superior air, she was getting too old to play with squirt guns anyway).

Gavin just smiled and took her hand. She could tell he was proud of her and happy to be home, and that was enough to make it all worthwhile.

• • •

After dinner, when the kids were all in bed and Gavin lay on the floor of the bedroom doing his evening routine of push-ups and ab crunches, Hannah stole out to the garage. It had been a big week, and she felt like her whole family had made a lot of progress in getting their lives on track, but one more thing still really bothered her.

So she made her way to the back of the dark, cobwebby garage and grabbed Gavin's fishing rod.

He gave her a strange look when he emerged from the bathroom, a toothbrush in his mouth, and found Hannah in the hallway with a fishing rod and reel, apparently trolling for codfish in the bottom of a heating duct. But as soon as she began to reel in her catch, he smiled in understanding. A moment later her wedding ring emerged from the grate. She took it off the hook and went to put it back on her finger, but Gavin stopped her.

"Whai. I'll oo ih," he said, his mouth frothing with toothpaste.

"What?" Hannah asked, laughing.

Gavin retreated into the bathroom, spit, rinsed his mouth, and returned. "I said wait, let me do it," he said.

Smiling, Hannah handed the ring over. Gavin took it and went to put it back onto her finger.

At the last second, she pulled away.

"Wait," she said, looking up at him. "You know I love you. You know our family is the most important thing in the world to me. And things have been good, they really have. But before I put this ring back on, I need you to promise me that I can trust you. That you won't lie to me. And that nothing like what happened with Nellie will ever, ever happen again."

He looked into her eyes. "I promise," he said simply. And taking her hand, he pushed the ring onto her finger. Then, still holding on to her, he led her into the bedroom.

# Chapter 12

◇◇◇◇◇◇◇◇◇

Saturday dawned bright and sunny. The sky above was a brilliant aquamarine, the birds sang, and the sun was warm on the bare skin of Hannah's arms. Gavin and Beau were inside, cuddled up adorably together and napping with a football game on the TV. Quinn and Sage sat on a blanket on the far side of the yard, playing together with their dolls in a rare moment of subdued, sisterly bliss. All the while Hannah lugged heavy bags of wood from the garage and spread them on the flower beds—a task she'd meant to do months before but had never found the time.

Another wife might have resented being out in the yard, slaving and sweating and performing manual labor while her husband satwas inside comfortably resting, but Hannah found outdoor work relaxing. Here she had no progress reports to fill out, no meals to make, no shopping lists to write, no emergencies to solve. She had only herself, the sun, the earth, and the bag of wood chips waiting to be spread. It was a feeling of divine, Zen simplicity.

As she dragged the bag over to the flower bed near the fence and spread the wood chips on the dark, moist earth, her thoughts drifted away on the wind that blew gently through the treetops. Her mind was so far away, she nearly screamed when a voice from the far side of the fence addressed her:

"You look awful pretty in that gardening hat."

Hannah dropped the handful of wood chips and jumped back from the privacy fence just in time to see Creepy Daryl's head appear over the top of it.

"God, do you always lurk behind fences and pop out at people like that?" Hannah asked.

Daryl gave her a smarmy smile. "Nope. Only for you."

"What do you want?" she demanded.

Daryl held up a page that appeared to have been printed from an Internet site. "I was about to buy these spy cameras from Tiger Direct—they got really good prices on them, but you get a discount if you order twenty. I was wonderin' if you might want to go in on 'em with me."

Hannah made a face. "No! Of course not. Why would I want to buy spy cameras?"

Daryl looked confused. "To keep an eye on your old man. Don't you remember? Him and my wife?" He slapped his hands together in a way that Hannah imagined was designed to simulate the sound of sloppy, slappy sexual copulation.

"Yes, I remember," she snapped with a glance over her shoulder. Fortunately Quinn and Sage were still on the far side of the yard, lost in their play, oblivious. Hannah approached the fence and spoke more quietly. "We've talked about it. We worked things out. Gavin's not going to be bothering your family anymore, and I'd appreciate it if you don't bother mine. We're healing and getting past what happened, and reminders don't exactly help—incidentally, neither do spy cameras. So thank you kindly for the thought, but I'm afraid I'll have to pass."

He gave her a pitying look. "A great man—Ben Franklin, or maybe Dr. Phil—once said, 'Once a cheater, always a cheater.'"

"No offense, Daryl, but my husband is not like your wife. And I am not like you. So thank you for the thought, but—"

Creepy Daryl gave her his creepy smile. "Oh, we just might be more alike than you think. I see you over here with your floppy gardening hat, your lonely little pink work gloves. I'll tell you one thing I learned a long time ago from an article in *Playboy* magazine: there is only one way to make things right with a cheating spouse. You gotta cheat yourself."

Hannah was done trying to be cordial. "Bye, Daryl," she said.

"We can start slow. A little online chatting. Maybe some sexting. Send a few pics back and forth."

"Ew!" she said.

He tried to say more, but she chucked handfuls of wood chips at him until he dropped behind the fence.

"Think about it!" she heard him say as he retreated toward the house. She hurled another handful at him as he mounted the steps that led to his back door, just for good measure.

• • •

The next day, on the way to work, Hannah's phone chimed. At the next stoplight, she looked at it and found a text from Tara waiting for her.

Hey girl, I need to talk to you.
Meet me at Hokey's Grill,
354 Pine Hwy. Rachel is
going to stay and cover
until you get there.

Hannah was a little confused by the short notice but excited about the prospect of catching up. She missed her best friend desperately.

When she had taken the job, she'd envisioned them working together every day and having the same sorts of good times they'd had during college, with trips to the beach, double dates, and late nights spent sipping wine and talking. As it was, she'd spoken to Tara only four times since she'd moved to Hickory Bluff, and only once in person. Most of those conversations had been spent with Hannah venting about Rachel's incompetence and sharing ideas for improving things in the company. Their visits were so brief and so dominated by business that Hannah hadn't even gotten around to sharing Gavin's heart-wrenching betrayal and their subsequent efforts to patch things up.

But now everything was different. She and Gavin were on the mend, and Hannah had mastered her job. She was eager to dish with Tara about her life and to talk about how she'd learned to reach the guys she cared for—and how that success could be emulated by other caregivers in Tara's company.

Excitement buoyed Hannah forward as she made her way through the vinyl-seated booths and 1970s veneered walls of the dive restaurant where Tara had suggested they meet. Even the strange décor and the odd-smelling, overall-clad men with the Amish-style beards and rock band T-shirts who ogled her as she walked in couldn't dampen her spirits—until she caught sight of Tara.

She sat in a corner booth, gazing at a half-empty coffee cup and meticulously tearing up her napkin, first into long strips and then into tiny, penny-sized shreds.

"Hey, girl!" Hannah said, using their usual greeting for one another.

Tara glanced up and gave her a smile that faded quickly. Hannah noticed right away that she looked bad. She had dark rings under her eyes, her hair looked thin, limp, and dull, and she wasn't wearing any makeup.

"Hey, girl. Sit down, okay?" Tara said.

Hannah sat, clutching her purse to her stomach for support the way Sage liked to hug her teddy bear.

"Tara, what's going on?" she asked. Clearly, whatever it was it was drastic, and there was no point in pretending to talk about anything else first.

Tara took a long time breathing in and then an equally long time expelling the breath. At the same time, she swept the snowflake-like shreds of napkin up into a neat little pile, then lifted her gaze to Hannah's.

"I have bad news," she said in a monotone Hannah found unnerving.

"Yes?" she prompted.

"I have a drug -addiction problem. It started when I fell off that porch in college and broke my ankle—remember? The doctor gave me Norco. Then I was having anxiety, so I started taking Ativan. From there the whole thing just...... got out of hand."

She opened her hands in a half shrugging gesture of helplessness.

"What do you mean *out of hand*?"

"I mean cocaine, pot. Heroin a few times. And lots of pills. Out of hand."

Hannah tried not to look as frightened and disgusted as she felt. "Jesus, Tara. Are you okay?"

"Yeah. I mean no," Tara said matter of factly. "Well, yes and no. I'm checking myself in to rehab."

Hannah nodded. She reached across the table and took Tara's hand. "Good, sweetie. That's good. What can I do to help you? I'll do anything. I'll visit you every day. I'll watch your cat."

"Thank you, Hannah. That's sweet. But really, I'm here to talk about the company."

Hannah paused, shifting her thoughts. Suddenly, in the fog of tragedy, she saw a glimmer of hope. "I can run the company while you're gone," Hannah said. "Or at least I can help. I've been doing so well, Tara. The guys love me. And I really love the work. These last few months, I've really gotten the hang of it, you know? And I have all these ideas about how we can make things even better. Trust me, Tara. Let me do this for you. Let me run the company while you're away."

But Tara shook her head. "You don't understand," she said. "There is no company."

Hannah recoiled, confused. "What do you mean?"

"It's bankrupt. Ruined. Gone. It's finished, Hannah. All the money, every penny there was, I snorted, smoked, shot up, or drank. No one's even getting a paycheck this Friday."

Hannah stared at Tara, too wracked with emotion even to blink.

"If there were still going to be a company, I'd let you run it, Hannah-bear. I would. But it's over. I'm sorry, girl. I'm here to tell you to start looking for another job."

• • •

On the way home from work that evening, Hannah made a call to Grandma Gem and asked her to keep the kids a little later than usual. Tara's news had hit her like an atomic shockwave, and she felt like she needed some time alone to process what had happened and make a plan. Most of all she had to figure out how to break the news to Gavin when he came back from his latest sales trip. Now, after all the struggles they'd been through to get themselves back on track financially, they were going back to square one.

She went home to a dark and empty house, thinking the silence and solitude would be a good balm for her aching soul, but only minutes after lying down on the couch she was sobbing. Wave after wave of emotion crashed over her, from frustration to anger to self-doubt to simple loneliness. At some point she must have dozed off, because when the knock at the door came, she nearly fell off the couch.

"Coming," she shouted. On her way to the door, she swabbed at the dried tears on her cheeks with one sleeve. It must have been later than Hannah imagined, and Grandma Gem was bringing the kids home—and Hannah didn't want her or the children to see her looking like a miserable mess.

But when the door swung open, neither a kindly looking old woman nor Hannah's children stood on the steps. It was a plump, pleasantly smiling African-American UPS man with a box under one arm. He glanced at the electronic package scanner in his hand.

"Uh, is Gavin Martin here?" he asked.

Hannah shook her head. "No. But I'll sign for it."

The driver hesitated. "Well, technically he's the only one who's allowed to sign for it. It specifically says so in the instructions."

Hannah blinked at the man. She was still waking up. "Well, I'm his wife, and he's not going to be back for a few days."

The driver made a pained face and glanced at the package, then at the electronic reader in his hand. "He's not, huh?" he said, seeming to agonize over the decision.

Hannah grew increasingly impatient. "It's up to you," she said. "Leave it with me or come back next week—I don't care."

The man sighed heavily. "Well, I don't want to have to come back. Just make sure he gets it, all right? Or my boss is gonna read me the riot act."

Hannah squiggled her signature on the electronic package reader and took the box, then headed inside, kicking the door shut with her foot. The sun had set, leaving the inside of the house so dark she had to make her way to the kitchen using intuition more than actual sight. Somehow she managed to set the package on the table without killing herself and turned on the light. She was just about to go to the fridge to see what there was to eat when she caught the scent of something in the air. It was sweet. Fragrant. Perfume.

She sniffed, and it only took a moment for her nose to lead her to the box. It reeked of some sort of drugstore knockoff scent, as if someone had deliberately sprayed it down with cheap perfume. The package itself was about one foot square, brown, and the address label was written in a loopy, florid female hand. The "i" in "Gavin" was dotted with a heart.

With a sense of steely, detached determination, she went to the block of kitchen knives, took out a paring knife, and attacked the tape.

In seconds she pulled the flaps back and stared down at the box's contents.

The first thing she found was a pair of red, lacy panties. She picked them up gingerly between her forefinger and thumb and brought them close enough to her face to see they had been worn, then dropped them onto the kitchen floor with a jerky movement, as if she were brushing a spider off her neck. She then proceeded to exhume the contents of the box one article at a time:

A large pink dildo.

A photo of a woman's crotch.

Three photos of a woman's ass.

Six photos of a woman's breasts.

A tube of heating personal lubricant.

A vibrating penis ring.

A silver stud of the sort used in pierced body parts.

A note: "Think of me. Xoxo, Kyra."

Three photographs of Gavin having sex with a raven-haired, tattooed woman. In two of them, the woman's arm was extended as if she were taking the picture herself. In the third one, Gavin's arm was extended. It was a self-portrait.

Hannah laid all the items out on the table and stood looking at them for a long time. When she grew tired of standing, she pulled out a chair, sat, and stared at them for even longer.

The tears she'd shed when she'd first arrived home seemed to have depleted her store of emotion, and she had none left now. What she felt as she stared at the sickening, horrific, disgusting, damning evidence of her husband's depravity was emptiness. Nothing else, just emptiness.

She gazed at the items for a few moments longer, until she felt she'd memorized them—until they were like the remnants of bright light, so burned into her eyes that when she looked away, she could still see them in front of her. Then, one by one, she gathered them up and put them back in the box. She carried the box out to the garage and put it on a high shelf, where the kids couldn't reach it. She came back in, washed her hands, then sprayed the kitchen table down with an industrial dose of Lysol.

Then she began frying hamburger for dinner.

By the time she called Gem on the phone, her voice sounded perfectly, almost eerily normal.

"Hey, Gem. You can bring the kids back whenever you're ready— and please feel free to stay for dinner if you want. Thanks again."

# Chapter 13

Today was a normal workday. The guys were engrossed with TV—except for Sebastian, who paid more attention to his robotic canine than the rerun of *Cops* with which the rest of the guys were enthralled.

Hannah sat at the dining -room table, absorbed with finishing up her weekly report. It was mind numbing and menial—she had to account for the petty cash, list the activities the guys had taken part in, and write a few paragraphs highlighting the progress each of them had made during the week. With Tara off getting herself clean and sober, Hannah didn't know who, if anyone, would read it, but she felt better when she was busy. Anything was better than dwelling on tomorrow, when Gavin would arrive back in town.

The talk he had coming was too big to have over the phone, so she'd spent their last few phone conversations talking to him in a tone that fluctuated between a detached monotone and fake, overacted sweetness. She still didn't know what she would—or could—say to him when she finally saw him face-to-face, but she had a feeling it wouldn't be pretty, which was why she preferred not to think about it.

A knock roused her from her work, and she went to the door in the same somnolent haze with which she'd done everything over last few days.

When she opened the door and saw the handsome man in the nicely tailored suit, however, she suddenly felt fully aware and present, as if a blaring alarm clock had jolted her out of sleep.

"Mr. LeVasseur! I didn't know you were coming today," she said.

"Bryan," he reminded her, straightening his tie and smiling as she ushered him inside. The guys greeted him with rapture, and he gave each of them a gift: a coffee-table book filled with pictures of famous paintings for John, a deck of playing cards for Ralph, and a set of binoculars for Sebastian.

Hannah watched as the guys were instantly absorbed in the gifts, and she was about to go back to her work when Bryan turned to her and offered her a small, wrapped package.

"One more gift," he said.

"That's not for me, is it?" she asked.

"Sure it is," Bryan said. "It would be rude to give everyone a gift but you, wouldn't it? Open it."

Hannah glanced at the ceiling, hoping that whatever deity existed above would help her keep the blush off her cheeks. Then, with a nervous laugh, she opened the package. Inside was a distinctive, light-blue jewelry box with "Tiffany & Co." in black letters on the lid. She gave Bryan a reproachful look, but his happy, open, slightly mischievous expression remained unshaken.

Hannah cracked the box cautiously, as if expecting a jack-in-the-box to spring out at her. After peering at the contents through the cracked lid for an instant, she opened the box all the way.

"Oh my gosh! It's beautiful. That's way too much," she said.

It was a lovely silver charm bracelet.

"What do you mean 'too much'? It has only one charm on it," Bryan protested playfully.

Indeed, Hannah found he was right. A single charm, a silver puzzle piece, was attached to one of the chain's links.

"I heard how you picked the perfect way to help each of these guys. That's what the puzzle piece is supposed to symbolize. You fit them. You found the right way to complete them, to make them happy. Anyway, there were no robot-dog or diaper charms, so that's what you got," Bryan finished, then gazed at Hannah, waiting for a response.

Suddenly she felt a wave of emotion. It wasn't the bracelet itself that moved her—although it was exquisite. Every day, from before dawn until eleven at night, she fought to make better lives for the guys at work, for her children, and for Gavin. Now, finally, someone seemed to have noticed.

"Don't take it the wrong way. I know you're married," Bryan said quickly. "Just take it as a token of thanks. I know how much you mean to my brother, and he means everything to me."

With some effort, Hannah squelched her happy tears and smiled.

"It's beautiful. Thank you."

Bryan took the bracelet out of the box, and Hannah felt a little breathless when his fingers brushed against her wrist as he put it on her.

"I really appreciate it, and I love your brother," she said. "I love all these guys—but . . . I don't know if you've gotten a letter from Tara or anything?"

"No," Bryan said. "Why?"

"Well . . . I have some bad news. I'm not going to be here anymore. The company is going out of business."

A look of shock registered on Bryan's face, followed closely by one of dismay.

"It has nothing to do with me," Hannah assured him. "I really like this job. It's Tara, the owner. She's going through some personal problems, and the company is apparently insolvent."

Bryan shook his head. "I don't understand. What are these guys supposed to do?"

"There are a few other companies around that do this sort of thing. I can e-mail you some links if you want," she suggested.

Bryan glanced at Sebastian, who gazed out the window at a bird with his binoculars and laughed joyously.

"Look, my brother has been through so many caregivers, I can't even begin to count. He's happier with you than he's been with anyone," Bryan said.

Hannah shook her head sadly. "I don't know what to tell you. I'm laid off. Tara already let me go. I doubt I'll even get paid for being here today. I just didn't want to leave the guys alone until other arrangements could be made."

Bryan's look of concern suddenly changed, and the mischievous glint returned to his eyes. He took a step closer to Hannah, and she tried to deny the pleasant nervous feeling she suddenly got in the pit of her stomach.

"Why don't *you* start a company?" he said.

Hannah blinked, her mind racing. The thought had never occurred to her until that instant. "Well, I . . . I've never owned a business," she said.

"You could do it. You're an intelligent woman. I've had my own firm for years. It's not rocket science—you just make sure you have more money coming in than going out, look for employees who care about these guys like you do, and you'll be golden. I'm not saying it will be easy, but I know you could do it. What do you say?"

"I . . . um . . . I don't know," Hannah said. The possibilities paraded across her imagination, filling her with an electric chill of excitement, but she didn't know how to feel. Could she do it? Was it even possible? She'd have to get licensed by the state, start a corporation or an LLC . . . .She'd need start-up money or at least a line of credit. But if she could get those things in order, she might be able to do it. No, not might—she *could* do it. She knew she could.

"Look, you start the company, and I'll be your first client," Bryan said, taking a checkbook out of his pocket. "I'm writing a check for Sebastian's care for the next six months."

"You don't have to," Hannah began, but he ignored her, and her protest faded.

His pen raced across the check in time with Hannah's racing mind. An instant later he ripped it out of the book and placed it in her hand.

Hannah looked at it for a moment, feeling scared and a little disoriented. In the next heartbeat, however, she steeled herself and decided.

"Mr. LeVasseur," she said, "it will be a pleasure doing business with you."

And she shook his hand.

• • •

Gavin returned from his business trip on Saturday afternoon to find everything in perfect order. The house was even more spotless than usual. Quinn and Sage were outside playing, and Beau was down for his nap. Fresh brownies cooled in a pan on the counter, and the house smelled like one of Gavin's favorite lunch dishes, homemade enchiladas, which were baking in the oven.

Hannah watched him enter the kitchen. He smiled at her and set his briefcase down by the door.

"Hey baby. Yum, smells like lunch in here," he said.

He made a move for the brownies, but something in the way she looked at him froze him in his tracks. Only then did he notice the cardboard box on the table.

"Sit down," Hannah said. She spoke quietly, but it was not a request. It was a command.

Gavin gave her a quizzical look and sat.

Wordlessly she pushed the box across the table toward him.

"What's this? Did my mom send us cookies again? I keep telling her you're a fine baker . . .." Gavin said, trying for levity. When Hannah did not smile, he opened the box. Hannah watched the color drain from his face as he reached in and rummaged around for moment, then pulled his hand out as if it had been stung.

"Jesus," he whispered.

He closed the box, pushed it aside, then wearily swiped his hands across his face.

"Hannah, I can explain," he began, but she cut him off.

"No. You can't."

Gavin gave a little sigh and stared down at the table, a little boy caught in a fib, waiting to be put in time out. It was pathetic. For the first time in her life, she found her husband, the man of her dreams, the father of her children, completely revolting.

"This is what's going to happen," Hannah said, her voice stony. "I'm moving to Salt Lake City and starting my own care business. The kids are coming with me. If you want to come with us and continue the pretense of our marriage for their sake, I won't stop you."

"Hannah, I swear, this will never happen again," Gavin began, but once more she cut him off.

"Our marriage is over, Gavin. I will never trust you again. I will never let you touch me again. But I know how hard divorce can be, and I swore I would never, ever put our kids through that. So if you can still live with me, knowing that I don't love you, that I don't even respect you anymore, then you can come with us. I don't need a husband like you, but our kids need a father."

"Baby, I'm so sorry. I'll make it up to you. I love you!" Gavin reached for her hand, but she jerked it out of his grasp.

"Don't touch me," she hissed. "I'm done with your lies and your excuses and your sick charm. All I want to hear from you is one thing. Are you coming with us? Yes or no."

Gavin drummed his fingers on the table for a moment then lifted his gaze to hers.

"Yes. I'm coming with you," he said.

Hannah rose from the table.

"Good," she said, her demeanor businesslike. "I'm going to go lie down for a while. Will you wake Beau up? And when the timer goes off, take the enchiladas out, okay?"

Gavin nodded, his eyes following as Hannah glided gracefully out of the room.

She passed down the hall, her head high, shoulders back, eyes unblinking. She stepped into the bedroom, shut the door, and locked it behind her. Kicking off her shoes, she climbed into bed and pulled the covers over her face.

Only then, alone and wrapped in a warm cocoon of darkness, did she finally release the strangled sob that had been building in her chest for the last two days. She sobbed until her sheets were soaked, her eyes puffy, her throat dry, her voice raspy, her muscles trembling. She cried until her whole body ached with the convulsions of her weeping, until she was exhausted, and finally until her tears had run dry.

Then she rose, went into the bathroom, washed her face, applied some makeup, and walked out to enjoy some enchiladas with her family—with a pleasant smile on her face.

# Chapter 14

◇◇◇◇◇◇◇◇◇

A week and a half later, Hannah stood in the center of a small, three-room office in Salt Lake City. She spoke into a Bluetooth headset to the parents of one of her new clients while simultaneously signaling to a pair of surly delivery guys, trying to show them where to put her new desk.

"Absolutely, Mr. Bernfeld. We provide twenty-four-hour supervision, meals, outings, and developmental therapy—all the services Compassionate Solutions did but at a 5 percent lower cost, and with a smile."

The furniture guys dropped the desk into place, nearly banging one of the freshly painted walls. Hannah cupped the earpiece with her hand. "Six inches that way," she said, pointing.

The delivery guys glowered at her but obeyed. On the phone Mr. Bernfeld was trying to get into the fine-print details of her services.

"Listen, I'll have my secretary e-mail over the contract, okay? Just give me a call if you have any questions."

The office chair was pushed into place now, while the second mover wheeled in a filing cabinet on a dolly.

"Knock, knock," someone said from the doorway, and she glanced over to see a short, stocky Hispanic man wearing a Yankees baseball cap. "I got your sign in the truck. Growth House, Inc., right?"

"Right. The big one goes on the door, the little one goes out front. I staked out the spot," Hannah told the sign guy. Then into the phone headset she said, "Bye, Mr. Bernfeld. Look for that contract within the hour."

She was glad to get off the phone finally; things were getting hectic. A glance at the new atomic clock on the wall told her that her next employee interview—the third of the day—would arrive in five minutes. *Good. That should just give me time to wrap things up with the movers and get the sign guy going.* She also wanted to get a thank-you note in the mail to the wonderful woman over at the bank who'd processed her business loan so quickly.

Her business plan had been simple at first: she'd logged on to the Compassionate Solutions computer system and begun calling up clients. They'd joined in droves, which had created problems and opportunities in abundance. With each new signed contract, she had more verifiable income. The problem was she hadn't been in a position to supply the services she'd promised. She needed capital to rent apartments and buy food for her clients, and she needed employees to staff the homes.

The new credit line ,had saved the day, and she'd immediately begun searching for staff.

Placing help-wanted ads and interviewing prospective employees was a laborious but rewarding process. Drive, intelligence, and honesty were traits she looked for, but kindness was what she prized above all else: an ability to treat her clients with love, to see the beauty in their human frailties and fall in love with it, as she had. Already she'd found several employees who she was sure would be great.

As she reflected absently on the last few weeks' trials, she dragged her new office chair into a corner and began typing up the promised e-mail to Mr. Bernfeld on her laptop—since, of course, she had no secretary.

All of this, every moment that had passed since she'd first decided to found Home Growth, Inc., had been a joyous chaos. She felt a hurricane of action surrounding her, and she was the center of it, the eye of the storm. But more than that, she controlled it. Her own will stirred the winds into motion, and her own decisions sent it churning in one direction or another.

It was, in many ways the loneliest, scariest, and most stressful time of her life. At the same time, she felt more herself than she ever had before. At last she was the captain of her own ship, the master of her own destiny. She was no longer looking to her father or Gavin for approval, or even for that elusive feeling called love. She was simply *doing. Being.* She was herself. And, for perhaps the first time in her life, being herself felt like more than enough; it felt amazing.

"I know we e-mailed the proof, but I thought you might want to see it in person before I hang it on the door," the sign guy said, fishing into a large, wax-paper envelope. He pulled out a thin, plastic sign with the Home Growth, Inc. logo Hannah had designed on it.

It was beautiful, and for a moment the overwhelming feeling of pride she felt stole her voice.

"Look all right?" the sign guy said.

"It's perfect," she replied.

But she didn't have much time to bask in the moment; already the one o'clock interview was at the door, and Hannah plunged ahead into her day.

• • •

Now, a month and a half to the day after Growth House had started, Hannah was spending a difficult morning wrestling with the new billing system. Her exhaustion complicated the task; she had been up until one1:00 a.m. the night before getting a payroll glitch straightened out. Her exhaustion and her focus put her in a sort of fugue state, and she knew from experience that she could spend hours immersed in her work and hardly come up for air. Now, however, an alarm beeped on her phone, and she sprang up from her desk.

"Shoot! Tara!" she said, and, snatching up her phone, she rushed for the door.

• • •

Sunlight Rehabilitation Center was a dreary-looking, gray cinderblock building with a tattered green awning. As Hannah pulled up to the curb, she saw Tara sitting out in front of it, using a small suitcase as a stool. She wore a pair of stained, velvet track pants and a baby-blue tank top thin enough to plainly display the zebra-striped bra she wore beneath it.

*Ah, Tara. Never one for subtlety.*

As she waited, Tara smoked a cigarette and spoke animatedly on her cell phone. When she saw Hannah getting out of the car, though, she ended the call and flicked her cigarette into the gutter, then swooped up her friend in a fierce hug.

"Thanks for picking me up, girl," Tara said, her words muffled by Hannah's hair. "I didn't want to see anyone's face today but yours."

When the two pulled apart, Hannah saw that Tara wasn't wearing makeup. Her hair was pulled back, and her face was scrubbed red. Hannah saw hints of crow's feet at the edges of Tara's eyes that she had never noticed before, and she wondered idly if she were showed the same signs of aging or if they were just the spoils of Tara's wild lifestyle.

Either way, Tara had always been the prettiest and most vivacious of her friends, and seeing her looking so weary was a little chilling.

Hannah forced herself to smile. "It's good to see you too," she said. "Come on, you want to get something to eat?"

"Ach, I'd trade my left ovary for a burger, some Tater Tots, and a cherry limeade. Can we go to Sonic?" she asked.

Hannah laughed, remembering the Sonic back in Springfield that had been one of their favorite haunts. "Sure. I think there's one on South Highland. Come on."

• • •

They sat in the car together, eating in silence except for the occasional screech of a straw and the rattle of crushed ice inside their Styrofoam cups.

"I just can't believe I fucked it all up," Tara said finally in weary amazement. "My aunt left me that business in her will. When I started running it, I thought it would be a new beginning. And I just pissed it all away."

Hannah looked at her friend, a gleam in her eye. "Well, it might not be completely gone," she said.

Tara glanced at her. "What do you mean? It's bankrupt. The employees were all fired. The clients were all cut loose. That's about as gone as it gets. Now I don't have a job, I'm broke—and I can't even have a fucking beer to wash down my hamburger."

Hannah turned in her seat to face Tara more directly. "What if I told you the clients aren't all gone? That there's a new company, in excellent financial health, that snatched them all up?"

Tara looked at Hannah, absently shaking the ice in her cup, a frown of confusion on her face. "What do you mean?"

Hannah offered Tara a business card that read: Hannah Martin, President, Growth House, Inc.

"I started my own company," Hannah said before Tara even asked the question. "Almost all the old clients signed on."

"That's . . . that's amazing," Tara said, but from the glazed look in her eyes Hannah could tell she wasn't exactly sure how to feel about the news. But that was okay. The part Hannah was most excited to tell her was still coming up.

"You know, it turns out that being the president of a company is pretty tough," Hannah said slowly, savoring the moment. "I'm up to my ears in work. I could sure use a good manager to help me out."

Tara's look of weary confusion dissolved into grin of disbelief.

"You mean—?"

"You'd have to stay sober."

"You're shitting me!"

"And I mean it, there's a lot of work. But if you want it, the job is yours."

Tara's squeal of delight was earsplitting, and she roped Hannah into another of her ferocious hugs. When she finally pulled away, tears glistened in her eyes.

"I won't let you down, Hannah," she said in earnest.

# Chapter 15

On Christmas Eve morning, Hannah came home from work to the trappings of the holidays: the smells of gingerbread, the fresh alpine scent of the Christmas tree, the twinkling of holiday lights, and the comforting croon of Bing Crosby singing "White Christmas" on the stereo. Her initial reaction was a sigh of contentment, but then she heard the chatter of little voices from the kitchen and winced.

All week she had promised her family she wouldn't be going into the office today. Unfortunately, she'd been forced to break that promise, and she was afraid the kids had been disappointed to wake up and find her gone. But what could she do? One of her staff had called in sick at the last minute. Everyone whose number she had at home was out of town, working, or refused to go in. So she'd had to go into the office and dredge up an old Compassionate Solutions phone list to find someone who could cover. She'd gone in at seven7:00 a.m., and it had taken her three and a half hours—plus paying the employee triple the standard rate—before she'd gotten someone to cover the shift.

But it was over now. She'd done what she had to do, and she refused to feel guilty about it. And now she had the rest of the day to make up for lost time.

"I'm home!" she announced as she entered the kitchen. She was greeted by a pair of sullen glances from Quinn and Sage, who both stood on chairs stirring a bowl of ingredients amid what looked like an explosion of sugar and flour. The only one who seemed happy to see her was Beau, who squealed happily at the sight of her. He was licking a big, wooden stirring spoon covered in pink frosting, which also covered his face all the way up to his hairline. He charged at Hannah, swooping in for a sticky-fingered hug, but she deftly turned him away from her dry-clean-only slacks and embraced him from behind. As she did, she pulled the slobbery spoon from his hand, which elicited a shrill cry of protest. Hannah looked around the room. Gavin was nowhere to be found.

"Where is your father?" she asked.

"On the computer, as usual," Quinn said with a roll of her eyes. The eye roll was getting to be a trademark expression of hers, and Hannah didn't like it.

"He let us bake cookies!" Sage said brightly, gesturing to a cooling tray full of charred black sugar-cookie remnants and another full of what looked like blobs of half-raw dough slathered with pink frosting.

"We didn't have enough red food coloring, so they turned out pink," Sage added sheepishly.

Hannah was already in motion, snatching a paper towel from the roll. She wet it, swabbed Beau's sticky hands and face, then snagged the next batch of cookies from the oven, which were already beginning to emit a foul black smoke.

"Gavin!" she shouted, trying to contain her irritation.

"You said you were going to be here this morning," Quinn said, her arms crossed over her chest defiantly.

"I know. I wish I was, believe me, but I had to go in to work. It was an emergency," Hannah said wearily as she embraced Beau, trying to stop his crying.

"You work all the time. Now the stupid cookies are ruined," Quinn said sullenly.

"No they're not! They're still good," Sage argued, and she snatched up a black cookie from the sheet and tried to bite into it—but it was so hard, it was like gnawing on a dog biscuit. She couldn't even break off an edge.

"We can make more, guys. I'll help you in a minute, okay?" Hannah said, and setting the now-pacified Beau down, she went down the hall in search of Gavin. She found him on the bed, still in his boxers and a tank top, messing around on his iPad. Hannah fought to contain the anger that sizzled up from her core.

"Gavin, what are you doing? The girls have just about burned down the house, Beau is covered in frosting, and the kitchen looks like a hurricane hit it."

Gavin looked up at her, his expression disdainfully blank. "What does it look like I'm doing? I'm job hunting."

"Job hunting, my ass," Hannah grumbled, kicking off her shoes and heading into the closet to change out of her work clothes.

"Well, excuse me, but I'm not the one who keeps uprooting the family and making us start all our networking from scratch."

"We both know how good you are at *networking*, Gavin. I'm sure you'll manage," Hannah said, pulling on her jeans.

"That's fine. Just keep dredging up the past, but I'm the one keeping this family together, Hannah. Ever since you started working in this business, you've been gone constantly. Since you started the new company, it's been worse than ever. You're just lucky you have me around to pick up the slack."

Hannah pulled on her shirt and came into the bedroom. "Oh, I'm lucky? Really?" she asked, incredulous.

"Sure," Gavin said. "You think the world is just crawling with husbands who are dying to stay at home and raise the kids while their wives are out getting their jollies as some kind of corporate ball busters? Someone has to raise the kids!"

Hannah stared at Gavin wide eyed. She couldn't believe what he was saying and was a little afraid that if she said anything at all, her response would be so caustic it would send him right out the door—and she didn't want the kids wondering where their father was, not on Christmas Eve.

"This is what you call raising the kids?" she asked when she'd calmed down enough to speak at a semi-normal volume. "They're running around like wild animals in there. If this is your supervision, Gavin, I'd be better off leaving them alone."

"Yeah, well, keep treating me like this, and that's exactly what you'll get to do," Gavin snipped, pulling on his pajama pants. She watched in amazement as he stormed off down the hall.

"Unbelievable," she whispered, wishing there were some audience present, some neutral party she could turn to and say, "See? See the crazy shit I put up with?"

But erethe only audience was the kids, and Gavin was probably out there with them right now, acting like Mr. Fun.

She let out what ended up being a half groan, half sigh, then made her way down the hall. The disaster-strewn kitchen was now abandoned, and the kids sat in the living room, sucking on Blow Pops and watching some vapid MTV show about crazy teenagers injuring themselves by doing stupid things.

Hannah glared at them all. "Quinn, change the channel. You know you're not supposed to be watching MTV. And no candy—it's not even lunchtime yet!"

"Dad lets us!" Quinn said.

Hannah had to bite her tongue almost until it bled to keep from making a snarky remark about their father. Instead, she redirected. "Let's watch something fun. I bet there are some Christmas cartoons on. *The Grinch*, maybe?"

With some cajoling, she managed to get the TV changed to an appropriate channel, then she set about cleaning up the kitchen.

*God, please just get me through the holidays.*

• • •

Alas, Christmas day was even worse.

Hannah had been up late getting the Christmas morning arrangements in order while Gavin put together a toy dollhouse for Sage.

They had spent the night vacillating between crabby banter and tense silence, and when they got to bed sometime after one1:00 a.m., Hannah had a headache, and her eyelids felt hot when she shut them.

She still slept in the same bed as Gavin so as not to confuse the kids, but after his last attempt, Gavin knew better than to try anything sexual with her. With him there but not there, she felt more alone than she had when he had been on the road and the bed was empty. In her state of irritation, she tossed and turned until after three.

At exactly 6:11 a.m. Sage came in and cannon balled into the bed between them, squealing "Merry Christmas!" at the top of her lungs. Quinn hopped up and down in the doorway, and Hannah could already hear little Beau shouting unintelligibly from his crib, apparently afraid he was missing the fun.

With a groan Hannah rolled out of bed and pulled on her bathrobe. Sage and Quinn led her to the doorway, each of them yanking one of her hands. Hannah glanced back to find Gavin still in bed.

"Are you coming?" she asked him, a little more pointedly than she'd meant to.

He grumbled something into his pillow and swatted at her, a dismissive gesture.

"Come on, Mom! We don't have to wait for Dad. We want our presents *now*!" Quinn said, and Hannah followed.

The ensuing hours passed as Christmas mornings normally did in the Martin household amid blinking Christmas lights, tearing wrapping paper, and sounds of the kids playing and running and shouting. Holiday songs blared from the stereo, and a big platter of coffee cake and doughnut holes lay out on the table.

After her miserable night, Hannah was tempted to wake up with some eggnog and rum, but she thought better of it and went with coffee.

At almost ten -thirty,when Gavin made his appearance, and he did so in grand style. The kids were all playing with their new toys at full throttle, and Hannah took advantage of the momentary parental lull by reading a few pages of the book she'd started back in May and had never had a chance to finish. When she saw Gavin standing in the doorway, though, the book nearly fell out of her hands.

He wore a Santa hat and beard and held a big, furry red sack in his hands.

"Ho, ho, ho! Who's ready for some more presents?" he asked in the worst Santa voice of all time. The kids all bellowed in excitement and barreled toward him. He handed out several packages to each of them, then settled down on the sofa next to Hannah.

"What are you doing?" she asked, her whisper tinged with suspicion.

"Oh, nothing. Just a couple more things a little elf told me the kids wanted," he said.

"Pocket princesses! Yes!" Sage shouted.

"The makeup set I wanted! Thanks, Daddy," Quinn said and gave her dad a big hug.

"Makeup?" Hannah exclaimed. She was loading up for a rant on the fact that Quinn was way too young for makeup, but Gavin gave her a wink.

"Dress-up stuff. It wipes off in five minutes," he said.

Beau gleefully played with a black plastic machine gun over by the Christmas tree-.

"Didn't we agree on no realistic guns?" Hannah demanded when she saw it.

Gavin gave a solemn nod. "I know, but all the guys are getting them. Eamon kept shooting him, and Beau was almost in tears. I didn't want the kid to be defenseless!"

"Who's Eamon?" Hannah asked, feeling bewildered and angry.

"Beau's best friend. From preschool," Gavin said as if it were obvious. But it wasn't. With the long hours she'd been putting in, Gavin had been the one to pick Beau up from preschool for the last two weeks. She'd practically had to beg him to do it.

Hannah was groping for a response when the doorbell rang. Doorbells reminded her of Gavin's infamous package, and the sound jangled her nerves. Even though she told herself she didn't care what sort of packages Gavin received these days, she rose quickly, unwilling to let him be the one to answer the door.

On the stoop she encountered a large, broad-shouldered man with greasy, slicked-back hair and a stubbly face, wearing a Denver Broncos jersey. He had one hand on the shoulder of a kid who looked a year or two older than Quinn. The boy had longish hair and the pretty, vaguely arrogant features of a Disney child star, the sort who graced the covers of *Tiger Beat* magazine. In his hands the boy held a small package with a tinsel bow.

"Can I help you?" Hannah asked.

"You must be the famous mom! I'm Don Branch," the man said and gave her an overly hearty handshake. Before she could react, the boy scooted past her and jogged down the hallway toward Quinn's room, his light-up sneakers blinking red with each step.

"Ah, young love!" Don said, and he moved toward her, clearly expecting to be invited in. "Say, I don't suppose you have any coffee brewing?"

The words "who the hell are you?" rose to Hannah's lips when Don's eyes drifted over her shoulder.

"There he is! The dean of the ninth green! Old short-stroke Martin!" he said.

Hannah found herself jostled out of the way as Don and Gavin came together in a fraternal handshake.

"Shut the hell up, man. I'm not supposed to be golfing. The wife thinks I'm at home baking cookies all day," Gavin joked.

Don feigned surprise. "You mean those snickerdoodles were store-bought? You sneaky son of a bitch!" he exclaimed, and the two men laughed.

"Come on into the kitchen. I've got a mean new craft beer for you to try," Gavin said.

Don nodded at Hannah as he passed her. "Merry Christmas."

Hannah was too frustrated and confused to answer. Instead she glared at Gavin.

"Can we talk for a second, honey?" she asked, the last word tinged with ironic venom.

"Sure. Just let me grab Don a beer and—"

"Now," Hannah interrupted.

Gavin gave Don a comical, wide-eyed *ooh, watch out for the bitch* look that made Hannah's blood boil.

She led him into the home office and used all her force of will to close the door rather than slam it. When she looked at him, Gavin had a look of disdainful boredom on his face.

"What the hell was that?" Hannah asked.

"Guests. And you were pretty damned rude," Gavin replied.

"Rude? I don't know them! They're strangers. This is my house. It's Christmas Day!"

"The guy is Don. We met at the reception after Quinn's school play. Remember? You had to cut out right after the bows to go back to the office to fix a QuickBooks glitch or something. He's a hell of a dude."

"Yeah," Hannah said impatiently. "And the kid?"

"The kid is his son, Jasper. Quinn's boyfriend," Gavin said.

Hannah gaped at him, momentarily too stunned to speak. "Boyfriend? Who said Quinn was old enough to have a boyfriend?"

"No one. She didn't ask our permission. They had already been boyfriend and girlfriend for a week and a half by the time I found out. Jasper is a sweet kid. He just dropped by to bring Quinn her Christmas present. But if you want to go in there and tell them they have to break up, by all means be my guest."

"Oh, you'd love that, wouldn't you?" Hannah said, her voice rising. "You just stay home all day golfing and showering the kids with candy, letting them break all the rules, and then when I finally get home from all the hours I spend busting my ass to make sure this family doesn't starve, I get to be the bad guy. Is that right?"

Gavin shrugged, giving Hannah that bored, arrogant expression she was growing to despise more and more. "I didn't ask you to start a company. I didn't ask to move to Utah. I liked our life in

California, Hannah. I liked having my wife at home. But it wasn't up to me, was it?"

"No," Hannah retorted. "The only thing that was up to you was whether or not to defile yourself with a string of sluts. And you did an excellent, excellent job of that."

"It's not my fault you're always working, Hannah," Gavin retorted. "If a wife isn't around, a man's eye's gonna wander. I'm sick of you blaming me for the problems you created."

His words hung in the air like a cloud of poisonous smoke, and Hannah fought for the breath to respond. Her whole body trembled with hurt and rage.

From outside in the hallway came, Don's voice: "Uh, hey Gavin? If it's not a good time, we can head out."

Hannah and Gavin's eyes locked. For a moment he looked almost boyish, like a kid begging for permission to go outside and play with his friends.

In an instant her bright, fiery anger deflated into something smaller and darker, an ember that fell into the pit of her stomach and lay there, burning her from the inside. She gestured to the door, a weary wave of permission and surrender.

Without another word Gavin left the room. She heard him greeting Don, his voice sounding eerily different from how it had a moment before—chipper, jovial, kind, charming—as if he were a completely different person. She wondered which was the real Gavin. It occurred to her in a painful jab of realization that she might never know. Worse, she might not even care anymore.

When the two men made their way back to the kitchen, Hannah ventured out into the hallway and made her way slowly down to the end, where Sage's room was. The door was ajar, and she peered in to find Quinn sitting on the floor with her boyfriend. Jasper was showing her a portable video game, and she watched over his shoulder as he played it. Occasionally one of them would pipe up with a comment on the action.

"What's that?"

"Those are Zorgats. The blaster doesn't work on them. You have to kill them with the plutonium suitcases."

"Ooh, cool—your guy has wings."

"That was an upgrade. It took me a long time to get it."

Their conversation was quiet and earnest, and it struck Hannah suddenly how grown up Quinn seemed in that moment. She had often been struck by how fast time seemed to move, but the feeling of vertigo it gave her now was more pronounced than ever.

Her little girl had a sweet, quiet, handsome little boyfriend—and Hannah had been the last to know. For a moment she wondered if Gavin's accusations might have a grain of truth. Was she too wrapped up in her work? Was she losing track of her family? Her husband? Was she losing herself? She tried to shake it off, but the idea, the guilt clung to her like burrs lodged in her heart.

Slowly and quietly she stole away from the door and headed into her bedroom. She climbed onto the bed and lay down there for a long moment, staring at the yellow light that shone in from the picture window and spilled across the ceiling.

*I am a stranger in my own house.*

*Gavin may be an asshole and a liar and a cheat, but right now it's like he's closer to the kids than I am.*

*Maybe Gavin and my dad and Trudy are all right. Maybe it is my fault. Maybe I'm just unlovable . . ..*

She stared at the ceiling for a long time, pondering her life, retracing the chances and choices that had brought her to that moment. In her imagination she gazed down forks in the road she hadn't taken and wondered what would have waited at the end if she had followed them. But in the end, her thoughts always returned to the present, to this moment.

Gavin wanted her to feel guilty, she now understood. He had ruined things, and now he thought if he could bribe the kids into adoring him, he could rewrite the past, make her into a villain and himself into a hero. She would not let that happen, she resolved. Even if that meant she had to leave him.

But despite the determination she felt, the guilt was never far behind, like a stalker hiding in the shadows, lying in wait to snatch her away.

She fell asleep for a while, and when she awoke, a pair of beautiful little eyes were looking into hers. At first she was startled, then she smiled.

"Hi there, sweetie," she said with a yawn.

Sage smiled back at her.

"Did you come to wake me up? You want me to come and help you put together your mermaid play kit?"

"I came to tell you you're the best mommy in the world," Sage said solemnly, "and Merry Christmas."

# Chapter 16

◇◇◇◇◇◇◇◇◇

A week later and Hannah was in the groove of work. She felt like a hummingbird, buzzing around at a mile a minute, zipping from one task to the next as if from flower to flower. It had taken a ton of effort, but the business was now taking off beyond her wildest expectations, and it was all she could do to keep up.

In that regard, Tara had been a big help.

She constantly referred to herself as "the new Tara," which was mildly annoying since she was only marginally less flaky than she'd been before rehab. But Hannah always enjoyed being around her, and Tara knew the business. It would have taken weeks of precious time to bring anyone else up to speed, but because of her experience, Tara was able to hit the ground running. Most of the time, she and Hannah saw eye to eye on things, and because of their long history they could communicate as intuitively as sisters.

Today Tara had been working on next week's schedule while Hannah was on the phone, closing a new client. When she finally finished answering the exhausting string of questions and ended the call, Tara was headed for the door.

"Oh, I was just going to grab lunch and run a couple of errands. You want to go first?" she said.

"No, go ahead," Hannah said. "I've got some stuff to finish up."

"You sure? You want me to pick something up for you?" Tara asked.

Hannah shrugged. She had too much to do even to think about food now. "I'm fine. See you in a bit," she said, and Tara headed out.

Hannah stared down at the flurry of papers on her desk, then clicked aimlessly around her computer screen for a moment. She glanced out the window and watched Tara's car disappear down the street, and then shook her head as if waking herself from a stupor. She glanced at the clock; it was one in the afternoon. She'd been in the office since seven7:00 a.m., and she hadn't eaten since six thirty. No wonder she was feeling like she couldn't concentrate anymore.

She thought about calling Tara and suggesting they grab lunch together, but on second thought decided it would be better to save money and head home for lunch. Besides, Gavin would be picking Beau up from day care soon, and if Hannah lingered she might get a minute of snuggle time with her little buddy before she had to go back to work.

The thought of soup, grilled cheese, and her sweet son had her smiling all the way home.

As she breezed into the house, she called out, "Gavin, you home?" The front door was unlocked, but she didn't see him until she turned the corner and looked into the living room. What she saw there stopped her dead. On one side of the couch sat Gavin. On the other side, so far away that she nearly melded into the armrest, was Tara.

Hannah looked from one to the other and back again. They were all silent, then they all tried to talk at once, then they all went silent again.

"Hey, honey, we were just—" Gavin began.

"Planning your birthday party," Tara finished, smacking her bubblegum. "Guess the surprise is ruined now, though. I thought you weren't going out to lunch."

"I thought you were going to a restaurant, not to my house," Hannah said.

"Well, happy birthday," Gavin said with a shrug.

Hannah eyed him. "My birthday is in a month and two days."

"What, do you expect us to plan it the day before?" Gavin asked.

"Yes," Hannah said honestly.

"Well, this is the new Tara," she said breezily. "I plan ahead."

She stood up from the couch. "I'm going to go powder my nose. "'Scuse me." And she left the room.

Hannah and Gavin were alone then, and he seemed to shrink under her gaze.

"What?" he asked defensively.

Hannah shook her head, but she didn't reply. The accusation that blared through her mind now was too horrible to put into words; the idea that she could be betrayed by the two closest people in her life was so far- fetched and so painful, she refused even to imagine it. And yet knowing Gavin, and finding them together like this, acting so strangely . . . As much as she trusted Tara, she found it hard to rein in her suspicions.

She heard a bang from the den then, and headed down the hall to investigate. She found Tara righting a table lamp.

"Sorry, bumped it," Tara said by way of explanation. She embraced Hannah and gave her an air kiss on the cheek as she slipped past her. "See you in the office, girl."

Hannah watched her walk away down the hall, then moved over to the armchair that sat beneath the lamp Tara had nearly broken. Slowly she sat.

Tara had said she was going to lunch, then she was here. Next she had said she was going to the bathroom, and Hannah found her in here, banging into the lamp.

She glanced at the lamp absently, and her eyes settled on the empty table beneath it. A picture of Gavin and the three kids had sat there; Hannah had it taken last year as a Father's Day gift. Tara must have knocked it over.

"She has to be drinking again," Hannah grumbled as she got down on her hands and knees and looked on the floor for the picture. But it wasn't under the chair or on the table or hidden under the hem of the curtain. It wasn't on the floor at all. She looked over the back edge of the table to see if it had fallen between it and the wall, but nothing was there.

The picture was gone.

• • •

Hannah tried her best to put the strange incident out of her mind, and found it surprisingly easy with all the tasks that confronted her every day both at work and at home.

She had expected things to level off with the company, but the business had surprised her by continuing to grow. Meeting the demand took a lot of effort, and even with Tara's help it was all Hannah could do to keep up. Things kept her on her toes at home, too. Gavin's moods were as strange as usual; most of the time he was aloof and caught up in his own needs, but sometimes he'd make romantic overtures that Hannah found mildly nauseating. Beau was a joy as usual, but he was getting more rambunctious as he got older and required more energy to corral. The girls always got along fairly well, but now that Quinn was thinking about boys, she sometimes fancied herself superior to Sage, and Sage was more needy than usual because of it.

All these things occupied Hannah's thoughts, so her days passed in a kind of frenzied, pleasant haze. On a Monday afternoon a week and a half after the lunch incident, Hannah and Tara were on their way back from Ogden, where they had been training new employees and helping set up a new group home. They were both exhausted and starving. They'd been working so hard, they'd neglected to eat lunch. So, as the car's gas gauge neared empty, Hannah suggested they stop and grab some Arby's.

Tara was behind the wheel. Driving, she claimed, was a Zen activity and good for her sobriety—which Hannah didn't mind as long as she kept the weightiness of her lead foot to a minimum. Now she swung off the highway, and the two women ordered food and coffee. Until the aroma hit her nose, Hannah had had no idea how hungry she was, but the minute she smelled it, she felt ravenous enough to tear the wrappers open with her teeth. She dug into the bag and fished out a few fries as Tara screeched up to a gas pump, nearly clipping it with her front bumper.

"Do you think you could—?" Tara began, but Hannah was already handing over her credit card. "Thanks," Tara said, and she got out of the car to pump the gas.

Hannah basked in the moment of peace, solitude, and silence. Fully dying of starvation now, she went to put her coffee in the center console cup holder, but Tara had it full of junk: gum wrappers, bobby pins, empty tubes of lip gloss, and cigarette butts. Rolling her eyes, Hannah reached up and set the coffee on the dashboard. It was fairly level, she reasoned. It should have been fine.

She had just reached into the bag to pull out her sandwich when she discovered that the cup was not level enough. It slid off and landed on her lap. Fortunately the lid stayed on or Hannah would have gotten a scalding bath. As it happened, she only got a minor shower, a spurt of coffee that belched out from the sip hole before she managed to snatch up the cup. It left a steaming brown stain on her beige dress pants, and already she could feel it soaking through and burning her.

"Shit," she exclaimed, holding up the dripping cup for a moment before deciding to set it on the floor between her feet.

Now to deal with the spill. She groped in the bag, looking for napkins. There were none.

Hannah groaned in irritation. Automatically she reached for the place where she kept spare napkins in her car: the glove box. But it was locked.

She reached over and snatched the keys from the ignition, inserted the key into the glove box lock, and turned. It popped open.

Instantly Hannah could see that there were no napkins inside; the box was nearly empty. What it did contain, however, made Hannah forget about the spilled coffee altogether.

She reached in, took it out, and slowly, and brought it toward her face. It was a framed picture of three beautiful kids, a boy and two girls, with their father. Hannah's kids, and Gavin.

Hannah stared at it in numb amazement.

Tara had taken the picture. But why? It was a bizarre mystery that even Tara's alcohol and drug addiction couldn't explain. What, was she planning to trade the picture for meth? Sell it for booze money? Not likely. What then? Why would she take it?

Hannah stared at the picture for a moment longer, then abruptly glanced around to see where Tara was. She no longer stood by the pump. Hannah looked ahead and caught sight of her through the gas station window; she was inside, coming out of the bathroom. Hannah watched her saunter up to the counter in her low-cut, silk shirt, grab a pack of gum from the rack, and slap it down. In an instant she'd paid the clerk and was heading out the exit, toward Hannah. Automatically, Hannah jammed the picture back in the glove box, locked it again, and then stuck the key back in the car's ignition.

She wanted to find out what was happening and why Tara had taken the picture, but she wanted to ask the questions on her own terms, after she'd had some time to think about it. Right now she was too tired, too confused, and too uncomfortable to focus, thanks to her hot, soggy pants leg.

"I got us some gum," Tara announced brightly as she got in the car. As they rolled out of the gas station, she turned the music up to a volume that made Hannah wince. But it was good in a way. Without music they'd have to talk. This way Hannah could stay silent and use the time to ponder what was happening. That was exactly what she did. The drive back to Salt Lake was sunny and scenic, but despite that, Hannah had a hard time repressing a feeling of doom.

Something with Tara was very, very wrong.

•  •  •

Hannah didn't get a chance to confront Tara about the picture that afternoon. Things were just too hectic. She intended to bring it up the next morning, but as soon as she sat down at her desk, she found a screen full of e-mails waiting. The accountant needed Genevieve's sSocial. The nutrition report had to be prepared for the state. Marilyn was training the new guy over in Hickory Bluff, and she needed a copy of the updated handbook printed and overnighted to them ASAP. The workload was so overwhelming, Hannah not only failed to confront Tara, she hardly even noticed when Tara sauntered past at noon and told Hannah she was going to lunch.

Hannah didn't look up from her computer screen until twelve forty-five, when someone pushed open the glass front door of the office, approached her desk, and asked, "Are you Hannah Martin?"

Hannah looked up at the visitor with eyes bleary from work and lack of sleep.

"Yes," she said. "Can I help you?"

The woman opened a folder, pulled out a packet of papers, and slapped them down on the desk.

Perplexed and annoyed, Hannah snatched up the papers and looked at them. The first words that jumped out at her were on the letterhead:

**State of Utah, Department of Health and Welfare.**

The next words she saw were:

License to operate as a care provider is hereby suspended until further notice.

Hannah's eyes snapped up from the page. For the first time, she looked closely at the woman. She wore an ill-fitting brown pantsuit, and her hair was pulled back in an unflattering bun. Her face wasn't encouraging. It was pinched and lined as if from years of frowning.

"What is this?" Hannah asked, the words coming out more forcefully than she intended.

"Your business license is being suspended, Ms. Martin. You are to cease all operations until the investigation is completed."

"Investigation into what?" Hannah demanded, her voice rising. This had to be a lie or a joke or a mistake. It couldn't possibly be true that everything she'd been working for was about to evaporate with a single packet of papers. "Investigation into what?" she repeated.

"Into the allegations made in this report by your employee. A Miss . . . ." The woman scanned her file. "Bennett. Miss Tara Bennett."

• • •

Hannah burst into the house and tore into the living room, her high heels cracking on the hardwood like gunshots. She knew the minute she saw Tara's car in the driveway that there had been no mistake at the State Department of Health and Welfare. Tara was trying to destroy her. And she thought she knew why.

In her emotional state, what she witnessed then came in fits and bursts of awareness: Gavin's wide eyes as he tried to push Tara off him. His shirt, unbuttoned. Tara's hand, tugging down her skirt as she shot upright and rose from the couch where she and Gavin had been sprawled. The mangled words as the two tried to talk over each other. Her own hands, balled up into fists and trembling. A thought: *I have never hit a person in my life. I can't hit her now. I can't hit him now. I can't hit anyone.*

Her voice screaming, blaring over their protests, their lame explanations.

"Get out!" she shouted over and over. "Get out, get out, get out!"

Then, all at once, like a summer thunderstorm's passing, the anger left Hannah. She was filled with a sudden, eerie calm. She had to distance herself from them, yes, but she also had to understand. More than anything, for her own sanity, she had to try to understand.

Gavin tried to talk again, but she hushed him. "Just answer my questions yes or no. And Ggod damn it, you'd better both tell the truth."

Tara tried to say something, but Hannah's fierce look silenced her.

"Have you been seeing her all along? When we were living in Hickory Glen, when you had to come up to Salt Lake on sales trips, were you seeing her then? Yes or no?"

"Yes," Gavin said quietly.

"Before that, in California?"

He closed his eyes in defeat. "Sure. A couple of times."

Her eyes shot to Tara. "You're one hell of a friend, you know that?"

"We're in love, Hannah," Tara shot back. "I tried to tell you. Even way back in California I tried. But I knew you would never accept it. You probably wouldn't even have believed that a guy like Gavin could be in love with me. You would have thought I was imagining things. You would have thought I was just jealous or out of my mind. Well, he should be mine, Hannah. Your kids should be mine. This house, this life—it should all be mine! It's obvious. I've know it all along. And then, when the stress of it gets to me, when I finally go off the deep end because of the fact that you're living this perfect life that should have been mine, and I turn to drinking and drugs— while I'm in rehab, you steal my fucking business!"

Hannah glared at Tara hard enough to ignite her. "All this time I thought you were my quirky, funny, over-the-top best friend. But really you're just a crazy, pathetic bitch," she said quietly.

Tara's normally pretty features twisted into an ugly scowl. "Yeah, well I'm the bitch who's getting your husband and your business, so suck on that," Tara said, and she fiercely snatched up her purse and stalked past Hannah toward the door.

"Tara," Hannah said, "you're not going to beat me."

Tara paused for a second, then snorted and charged out the door.

Now it was just Hannah and Gavin. Immediately he slipped off the couch and fell to his knees.

"Baby, I'm sorry. But you've been working so damned much. I'm a man. I'm a human being. I have needs."

Hannah stopped him with a gesture. "I have needs too. Right now I need you to get the hell out of this house."

"But . . . ,." Gavin stammered. "The license thing. I know Tara made up the accusations. I could help you."

"I don't need your help," Hannah said. "I will beat Tara, and I will keep my business, but I'll do it without you."

"Hannah, baby, be reasonable. Any man who's out on the road all the time—"

"Gavin, I'm counting to three. If you're not out of the house when I'm done—"

"Then what? It's my house too," Gavin said.

"Use your imagination," Hannah growled. "One . . .."

"Sweetie, we can work this out."

"Two . . .."

"I just need you to be more attentive to my needs, then I won't have to look elsewhere. If you weren't working all the goddamn time—"

"Two and a half," Hannah said.

Gavin opened his mouth to utter a protest. He shut it again. Something in Hannah's eyes told him it would be very dangerous to push her any further. Gavin was a bold man in some ways, but he wasn't stupid. There was an old saying: you mess with bull, you get the horns. He was about to get the horns—big time.

As soon as he realized Hannah wasn't going for his bullshit, Gavin deflated. His head drooped, his shoulders stooped. Slowly, like a pouting kid, he slunk from the room. Hannah listened as he went through his drawers upstairs, heard the familiar zip of his luggage, followed the sound of his feet drumming down the steps again, then finally registered the clunk of the front door shutting behind him.

She felt two feelings at once, both of them overwhelming enough to bring her to tears. One was a loneliness that shivered her entire body like an orgasm; the other was a relief so sharp it filled her with aching.

It was done. She had done it. Gavin was gone for good.

# Chapter 17

◇◇◇◇◇◇◇◇◇

The next morning Hannah sat in the reception area of a modern, stylish office. Lovely abstract paintings hung on the walls, the canvases bathed in cascades of colors that tumbled together like the interplay of light through boughs in a forest. In fact everything, from the spare yet comfortable leather chairs to the triangular coffee table made of some sort of exotic-looking hardwood, had a feeling of art and sophistication. She appreciated the beauty of the space, but it made her feel a little uneasy too—the way Cinderella might have felt if she'd gone to the ball to beg the prince for pro bono legal representation.

After a few minutes, footsteps approached from down the hall, and then Bryan LeVasseur appeared, wearing his customary suit and his disarming smile. Hannah rose quickly. For some reason she was so rattled by his sudden appearance, she almost launched into her pre-rehearsed explanation of the facts right there. But before she could, Bryan took her hand in both of his, cupping it between his palms like a bird he'd caught.

After the tortured, sleepless night she'd spent and the agony she'd gone through debating whether or not to call him, his simple gesture almost brought up grateful tears.

"You okay?" he asked.

She nodded.

Bryan led her back into his office. It was as nicely decorated as the lobby, but on the walls hung a series of old photographs. They looked like still shots from 1920s-era silent films and featured silver-and-black rendered heroines with darkly made up eyes, set in various poses of seduction, despair, or delight. She glanced from one of them to the next, then finally to Bryan, who settled into the chair behind his desk.

What sort of a man was he? He had been so kind to his brother, so polite and friendly to her. Clearly he was a successful attorney. Now here was another wrinkle—was he artistic too?

He noticed her looking at the pictures.

"Stills from the set of an old Von Stroheim film," he said, then by way of an explanation added, "I'm a big movie nerd."

Hannah couldn't help but smile. "Yes, I thought so. *Nerd* is always the first word that comes to mind when I think of you," she teased.

Bryan laughed. "But enough about me," he said. "What can I do for you?"

Hannah took a deep breath, then unreeled all of it. She told Bryan the whole story, from her move to Hickory Bluff and Gavin's infidelity to her triumph creating the new business and finally Tara's betrayal.

When she finally finished, Bryan gave a low whistle.

"That's quite a story," he said. "So step one, you need to get your license reinstated—fast."

"Yesterday, if possible," Hannah agreed.

"Do you have the document the lady from the state gave you?"

Hannah took it out of her bag and laid it on Bryan's desk. He examined it, rubbing his fingers across his lips as he did, in a gesture that Hannah tried not to think of as erotic. After a moment, he looked up at her.

"Well, it's pretty straightforward. We just have to march into that hearing next week and prove that all the charges are baseless. I presume the company's books are in order?" he said.

"Perfectly. I'm crazy meticulous. But—"

"What?"

Hannah winced as she said it. "Until I get the license back, my cash is completely tied up. I have rent to pay, payroll to meet. I was thinking that maybe you could refer me to a free legal aid attorney or something, but—"

He laughed. "Give me a break."

"Bryan, I'm serious. I have no money to pay you."

He smiled that warm, intense smile of his. Seeing it felt like stepping into the sun.

"Good," he said. "I wouldn't accept your money anyway."

At that moment Hannah understood what kind of man he was. Still, she had never accepted charity in her life, and she wasn't going to start now.

"No deal," she said. "How about this: you write up a payment contract, and we'll do it in installments."

Bryan raised his eyebrows. "You drive a hard bargain, Hannah. Deal."

•   •   •

At eight o'clock the following night, Hannah and Bryan sat in the office of Growth House, Inc. eating take-out Chinese food straight from the cartons. Bryan had traded in his beautiful suit for a more casual look—jeans and a V-neck T-shirt, through which Hannah couldn't help but notice his muscular arms, athletic chest, and (she imagined) stony abs. The kids had been there since they'd gotten out of school, too—and they had been growing increasingly restless.

"Here. Angry Birds," Bryan had said to Beau when he'd started to throw a fit, and he'd generously handed the boy his phone, pacifying him.

But the girls had been showing signs of irritation and exhaustion too.

"Why can't we watch TV?" Quinn had demanded.

"Because there is no TV here," Hannah had said. "And we can't go home because I have to get this very important work done, okay? I need you to be a big girl and play with your sister."

"Where's Auntie Tara?" Sage asked. "Last time she came over, she promised to paint my nails, then she didn't come over again."

*Auntie Tara is a psychotic whore*, Hannah replied silently. Aloud, she said, "I promise we'll paint your nails this weekend, okay? But Mommy and Bryan have a lot to do right now."

That had satisfied her, temporarily at least.

Following Quinn's final, brief outburst at having to eat "yucky" takeout Chinese food, the kids had retreated to the makeshift playroom in Tara's old office. For the last twenty minutes or so, they had been quiet, and Hannah was grateful for the reprieve.

Now Bryan scanned a bank statement, his finger tracing quickly across lines of numbers. Stacks of papers and files sat mounded around them. They'd been at it since nine that morning: sifting through the files, printing e-mails, and gathering all the necessary evidence to counter Tara's accusations.

Hannah had already put in seventy hours that week, making sure the paperwork and the books were in order in preparation for Bryan's visit. To say she was exhausted would have been the understatement of the decade, but she knew the work was far from done.

Bryan was just flipping to the back page of the statement when his cell phone buzzed.

"Hey Tony, what's up?" he answered. Tony, Hannah knew, was one of Bryan's partners at the law from. "Yeah, I'm with her now," he said with a glance at Hannah.

He listened to Tony for a moment, and his customary smile disappeared. "Uh-huh . . . .Uh-huh . . . .Wow. All right, e-mail me all the documentation you have on it."

He ended the call and looked at Hannah. The expression on his face stirred a wave of fear in her.

"You want the good news or the bad news?" he asked.

"The good, I guess," Hannah said.

"It looks like BYU is going to have a pretty good football program this year," he said, ending his joke with a wan smile.

"And the bad?" Hannah asked.

Bryan drew a deep breath. "Well, it looks like your buddy Tara has friends in high places. Specifically an aunt who's a state senator. She's the one who's lobbing all the allegations of abuse and neglect at you."

"So what does that mean for us?" Hannah asked, her heart in her throat.

Bryan shifted in his chair. "Well, it explains why the Department of Health and Welfare yanked your license before even bothering to investigate the allegations. It's never good to have enemies in high places. But basically it doesn't change things much. There are tons of witnesses willing to testify on your behalf, and your recordkeeping is bordering on obsessive compulsive—which we lawyers love, by the way."

Hannah smiled. As much as he was doing for her, the thing she appreciated the most was his ability to make her smile no matter how bad things got.

"So . . . ?" Hannah prompted.

"I never make promises to clients," he said. "But as a friend? Don't worry. I'm going to take care of this for you."

Their eyes locked, and the gaze lingered, as if he didn't want to look away any more than Hannah did. Finally he glanced down at his watch.

"I should probably head out."

"Right. I'd better get the kids to bed," Hannah said quickly.

She rose from her chair while Bryan gathered his notes and put them in his computer bag, then she walked him to the door.

Before leaving, he turned back to her and placed a hand on her shoulder. She felt herself stiffen at the touch, then, as she relaxed, warmth shot through her from her toes up to her heart.

"It's going to be okay," Bryan said. His gaze held her for a few seconds, then he squeezed her shoulder, released it, and left.

Hannah watched him leaving for a long moment, her mind abuzz with questions. Was he just helping a friend in need? Did he still feel the way he had when they'd first met and he'd brashly asked her out? Did he have a girlfriend now? Most of all, what on earth was going on between them? *I mean, a shoulder squeeze? What does that mean anyway?*

Hannah remained lost in thought for a moment, then shook herself out of it. She had a business to protect, a court case to win, divorce papers to file, and three kids to put to bed. She had no time to ponder love.

With a long sigh, she turned from the door. She began tidying the stack of papers she'd been working on, then decided to leave them for the morning. Shouldering her purse, she walked into Tara's old office to collect the kids.

She found them lying on the floor in one corner on Beau's blue quilt, cuddled together like a litter of sleeping puppies. Once again, in the midst of the greatest crisis of her life, Hannah smiled.

# Chapter 18

◇◇◇◇◇◇◇◇◇

Hannah sat on the couch, poring over her mounting legal bills. She couldn't pay them, and unless something changed soon, she wouldn't be able to buy food either. The whole thing made her stomach cramp and twist with anxiety.

The business had been shut down for a month now. Two weeks ago she'd had to give up the lovely brick townhouse she had rented due to the catastrophic state of her finances. Now she sat in a cramped two-bedroom apartment with boxes stacked high around her. Between preparing for the upcoming court appearances and taking care of the kids, she'd had no time to unpack. And it wasn't as if there were enough closet space in the tiny flat for her to put their stuff away properly anyway.

Without taking her eyes off the page, she reached over, grabbed a tissue from a box, and blew her nose. As if things weren't bad enough, she'd been sick for the last week too.

Despite the suffering she'd experienced in the last couple of weeks, the loneliness she felt today was the worst trial of all. The kids were at Gavin's for the weekend. Her heart ached without them, almost worse than the pain that radiated through her stuffy, pounding head. But she knew that no matter how big an asshole Gavin was, he was still the kids' father, and she wasn't going to stand in the way of their seeing him now that he'd finally expressed an interest in having them visit.

She'd been tempted to ask him if Tara would be there but managed to restrain herself.

Hannah sighed and placed the bills neatly on the table with the rest of them. She entered the total into the calculator and looked at it for a moment. Only two weeks, and her legal bill was astronomical. For a second she almost wished she'd taken Bryan up on his offer to work on her case pro bono, but she reminded herself that wouldn't be right. She hadn't known him that long, and it would have been too large a gift to accept, even from someone who was fast becoming a good friend. Besides, she reasoned, she'd have the money to pay him back soon—as long as she didn't starve to death first.

The doorbell rang. Startled, Hannah shot to her feet. It was only Tuesday, wasn't it? Bryan wasn't supposed to come by until tomorrow. She raced to a mirror, ran her fingers through her hair, and slathered on some lipstick, then rushed to the door.

When she opened it, however, she saw immediately that it wasn't Bryan. It was a tall, skinny teenager in an FTD florist shirt.

"Delivery for Hannah Martin," he said, his voice cracking mid-sentence.

She politely accepted the delivery, tipped the kid, took the flowers inside, and read the card.

Baby,

I miss you. If you can forgive me, I can forgive you.

Let's work things out.

Love and smooches, Gavin

Hannah didn't even glance at the flowers. She didn't laugh or cry or scream. She simply walked calmly to the garbage disposal and turned it on. She stared down into the black hole at the bottom of the sink for a minute as the vibration from the machine rattled the glasses in the cabinet and made the floor seem to buzz under her feet. It was a frightening sound. A sound of destruction and chaos and loss. She listened to it a moment longer, then jammed the flowers into the garbage disposal and watched as the hole ground and gobbled them up, card and all.

• • •

Now ten-thirty at night, the kids were asleep. The apartment was quiet save for the ticking of the clock on the wall and the faint drip-drop of rain outside the window. Hannah sat on the couch, staring at her cell phone. After a long moment, she finally selected the number and hit talk.

It rang, then rang again. Finally a voice answered, its timbre low, gravelly, and familiar.

"Hello?"

Immediately she thought of the little speech she'd written in her head earlier.

*Listen, Dad, I have a problem. Gavin and I are separated. Before it happened I started a wonderful business. I worked so hard to do it—you'd have been so proud of me—but Gavin's girlfriend wrecked it all. It was my ex-friend Tara, if you can believe it. Now I have nothing. No income. Barely any savings. A pile of legal bills. Dad, I know I haven't asked anything of you, not since I was a kid, but . . . I need your help. Just a little money to get me through. To pay the rent. To put some food on the table for the kids. To get Beau his Pull-Ups. Dad, I swore I would never ask you for anything, but this is different. I'm really desperate. I have no one else to turn to. Nowhere else to go. I'm scared, Dad. I need you. Because if you don't help me, I have no one to rely on. I have no one else, Dad. No one but myself.*

The speech unspooled in her mind, but she didn't say a word aloud. It was as if she couldn't, as if her vocal cords were frozen in her throat.

"Hello?" her father said again.

She sat in silence for a moment, listening to him breathe. She even opened her mouth to speak, but again she didn't.

"Hello? Hannah?"

*No. I swore I'd never ask him for help. I'm not doing it now. I've gotten this far on my own. I can make it a little bit further.*

She ended the call.

That night she lay in bed, staring up at the blue lines the vertical blinds painted on the cracked ceiling of the apartment. She lay awake for hours.

•  •  •

Wednesday was the day she looked forward to all week: Bryan's visit. Even though she was still sick, the thought of it was almost enough to make her feel healthy. All morning she bustled around the house nervously. She showered. Dressed. Changed, then changed again into something nicer, then changed again into something more casual. After all, this was a business meeting, she reminded herself sternly, not a date.

Still, when the doorbell rang, there was no denying how fast her heart started pounding. Or maybe that was just the massive sinus infection . . ..

"Special delivery," Bryan said, brandishing a paper bag.

Hannah looked inside and, for the first time all day, the pall of her miserable cold lifted. Bryan had brought a care package for her complete with hot herbal tea, steaming chicken-noodle soup, a box of animal crackers, a bag of cough drops, and in case all that wasn't strong enough for her, a bottle of wine.

"You don't have to do all this for me," Hannah said over their little feast.

"Don't worry. I'm an attorney. It will all show up on your final bill," he said and gave her the mischievous grin she'd come to expect from him. She found an interesting contrast between him and Gavin. Gavin was always trying to act like he was perfect, but he was constantly doing rotten things, while Bryan could smile and flirt with the devil's charm, but deep down he was incredibly patient and kind. At least he'd always seemed that way. After what happened with Gavin, she suspected, it would be hard for her to trust again soon—maybe ever. But she couldn't deny the fact that aside from spending time with her kids, Bryan's visits had become whats she looked forward to most every week.

"So, tomorrow is the big day in front of the judge. How are you feeling?" Bryan asked, then took a spoonful of his soup.

"Nervous," Hannah said. "How are you feeling?"

Bryan paused, considering the question. "Pretty good, all in all. I just wish we had some way to establish Tara's motive for telling all these crazy lies about you. You can tell the judge you found her with Gavin, of course, but it will just be your word against hers. If we had solid evidence, it would be an open-and-shut case . . . It will work out anyway, though. Don't worry. You haven't done anything wrong, and the judge will see that. We hope."

Hannah crunched on an animal cracker. Bryan went into talking about something else, but she didn't hear him anymore. Her thoughts were far away—eighty-five miles away, to be precise. He had given her an idea.

•  •  •

Hannah stood on the front stoop, breathing in the chill, crisp air. It made her cough, and she sifted a half-soggy tissue out of her pocket and blew her nose. The stress of her predicament was having a major effect on her health, no doubt about it. But now she had an idea of how she might take control of her situation.

Her plan was fairly desperate, to be sure, but at least she was meeting her fate head- on instead of waiting passively like a victim. Whether her idea worked or not, taking action had given her a newfound sense of hope and power that made her feel slightly better despite the fact that she was sick, exhausted, scared, and in Hickory Glen.

When she'd lived there, the place had seemed like a special level of hell, but now that she had left, she felt a strange nostalgia for it. This place had been the start of a lot of things for her, she supposed. The start of her business. The beginning of her understanding of who Gavin really was. And even though she'd had a fairly miserable time here, she would never forget Hickory Glen.

She knocked on the door again. From inside, she heard the sound of a child wailing, the TV blaring, and finally heavy footsteps coming toward the door. It opened to reveal the face of an old friend.

"Hi, Creepy Daryl," Hannah said.

If the nickname bothered him, he didn't show it. "Well, if it ain't my favorite ex-neighbor," he said, grinning, then he raised one eyebrow in a comically seductive expression. "You here to take me up on my offer finally?"

"Yes," Hannah said.

His face lit up like the Fourth of July.

"Not that offer, you perv," she amended quickly. "I want to borrow some of your spy cameras."

# Chapter 19

◇◇◇◇◇◇◇◇◇

On Monday morning Hannah sat in the courtroom. It was a bland place with wood-paneled walls. where tThe judge sat on a dais, with the state of Utah seal on it. A large, African-American clerk sat at a desk below him, typing something into an outdated computer, a scowl on her face. The few people in the room included a couple of balding lawyers in ill-fitting suits, a shady-looking guy in a dirty, torn polo shirt, and an old woman in a green jogging outfit with a fat manila folder under one arm.

Hannah took it all in, chewing on a piece of gum so hard she thought it might disintegrate in her mouth. All the stress; all the preparation; all the sacrifice; all the work, time, and effort she and Bryan had put in—all of it had come down to this.

She heard the door opening and glanced across the courtroom. A woman in a blindingly bright fuchsia skirt and blazer entered and sat across the aisle across from Hannah. It was Tara. A moment later Gavin came down the center aisle of the courtroom and sat down next to her. Gavin! How could he be there? How could his betrayal be so deep, so complete? The sight of him sent Hannah's soul roiling with fury, and she fought to steady herself.

She felt a gentle hand on her shoulder and glanced at Bryan.

"It's all right. We've got this," he said reassuringly.

He was right. Tara might have Gavin, but Hannah had Bryan on her side. Plus she had an ace up her sleeve.

•  •  •

The lawyer from the state called his first and only witness, Tara Bennett, to the stand. She rattled off a whole litany of charges for half an hour. Hannah abused the residents in her homes. She embezzled funds from her company. She evaded taxes. She hired illegal-immigrant workers. She destroyed pertinent documents. She stole money from her clients. She defrauded Tara by stealing her business. The judge, a middle-aged man with a bowtie and an Amish-style, moustacheless beard, raised his eyebrows at each new accusation. The charges were ridiculous, every last one of them, and Hannah and Bryan had spent the last month putting together all the necessary documents to refute them. But still Hannah had to fight the urge to spring from her seat and shout, "She's lying!"

Twice Bryan put a hand on her forearm to calm her.

When it came time for cross-examination, Bryan did a good job of poking holes in Tara's story, then he presented more than two hundred documents to the court record showing that everything Tara had said was false.

"That's all well and good, Mr. LeVasseur, but if all these charges are unfounded, why would she make them in the first place?" the judge asked.

Bryan cleared his throat. "Well, first of all, Your Honor, she believed my client stole her business."

"But Mrs. Martin gave her a job, did she not? According to the documents the state submitted, she was making as much money working for your client as she had when she'd owned her own business. Why would she upset the apple cart unless she was doing it in the interest of the clients, as a concerned whistle blower?"

Bryan adjusted his tie. "That's true, Your Honor. Ms. Martin did give Ms. Bennett a job. But Tara Bennett was also having an affair with Mrs. Martin's husband, Gavin. He's sitting right next to her today, in fact," Bryan said and pointed at the couple.

The attorney from the state sprang from his seat. "Mr. LeVasseur's accusation is completely unfounded, Your Honor. Mr. Martin and my client have been friends for many years, and he's here to support her during a difficult time, nothing more. Mr. LeVasseur has no evidence to support his assertion, and I move that it be stricken from the record."

The judge's overactive eyebrows rose again. "On the contrary, if Miss Bennett and Mr. Martin were having an affair, I think it would be very pertinent to this matter. Mr. LeVasseur, do you have any evidence to back up your claim?"

Hannah watched as Bryan's shoulders slumped. "No, your honor," he admitted.

"Yes!" Hannah corrected, and she jumped up from her seat. With a sidelong glance at Tara and Gavin, she strode to the front of the courtroom, took a flash drive from her pocket, and handed it to the clerk.

"This is the evidence?" the judge asked.

"It's a video, Your Honor," Hannah said.

"At last things get interesting," the judge quipped, then to the clerk he said, "Candice, get it up on the big monitor, will you?"

For a long moment the flat-screen TV that sat in one corner of the room remained black. Then it flickered on, and there were Tara and Gavin in Tara's bedroom. She was on her hands and knees, wearing a tangerine-colored lace teddy. Gavin was behind her, his bare chest slick with sweat. His face was scrunched up, and his tongue stuck out one corner of his mouth in an expression that looked like a cross between concentration and pain. He thrust his hips spasmodically and grunted.

"Oh God! Oh God!" he said, his mouth suddenly gaping like a codfish's.

Tara held a riding crop in her hands, and she occasionally reached back and slapped Gavin on the thigh with it, hard enough to make him wince.

"Harder, you little bitch! Harder!" she commanded. "Fucking make me feel it."

A booming laugh came from the judge's bench.

Gavin had doubled over, his face cradled in his hands. Tara remained upright, but she shrunk down in her seat slightly, her face deathly pale.

"Fast forward to the next part. Five and a half minutes in," Hannah said.

The clerk nodded and skipped forward.

On the screen, Gavin and Tara were now cuddled together in the sheets in a state of sleepy, post-sex bliss.

"I don't know," Gavin drawled. "She's worked so hard. It just seems harsh to make up all these lies about her and ruin her company. Why don't we let her keep it, and I can just collect alimony or something?"

Tara slapped him hard on the bare chest. "Because we'll make way more money if I can reopen my company and take over all the business she's built up, idiot. Besides, all these years she's kept you from me . . . .I want that smug slut to suffer."

Gavin shrugged. "Fine. I don't like to lie, but I support you, sweetie. Whatever you want."

"Damn right," Tara said, and she pinched his nipple so hard he groaned.

The judge waved his hands, and the clerk paused the video.

"Enough!" the judge said. "As much as the state of Utah enjoys a good smutty movie, I'm afraid we have other business to attend to."

He looked at the attorney for the state, whose face was red with embarrassment or anger.

"Counselor, you have anything to say to that?"

"No, Your Honor," he said so quietly he could barely be heard.

The judge looked at Tara.

"What about you, Miss Bennett? Anything to add, or does that video basically sum it up?"

Tara looked like she was about to speak, but the judge spoke first.

"You know, lying in a court of law is called *perjury.* It can land you in jail, Miss Bennett. What were you about to say?"

Tara's gaze fell to her feet. She shook her head.

The judge sat up in his chair. "All right then. The court hereby orders that Growth House Incorporated's license be reinstated effective immediately and that all charges against Hannah Martin be dropped. Case dismissed."

The gavel clacked, and Hannah felt Bryan's arms come around her in a bear hug. It took a moment for it to sink in. The terrible ordeal had finally passed. She had won. It was over.

●  ●  ●

Hannah stepped down from the marble courthouse steps into the sunlight. It was cold, but the sky was a vivid blue, and chirping birds darted here and there across the bright-emerald lawn of the courthouse square. Hannah felt like she'd been released from prison after a twenty-year stay. It was glorious. But her work wasn't quite done.

She looked for Tara and Gavin and found them almost immediately. They stood a few yards away, under a towering bronze statue of Brigham Young. They were fighting. As Hannah watched, Tara cursed at Gavin and stormed off across the courtyard. Gavin went to stalk away in the opposite direction, but Hannah called out to him. She wasn't done with him yet.

"Hey Gavin, wait up," she said, sounding more cheerful than she'd felt in a months.

Gavin stopped. "What?" he asked warily.

"I have a surprise for you," Hannah said. She turned around and shouted. "Hey ladies, come on out!"

From around the corner of the courthouse, came a stampede of more than two dozen women. High heels rattled down the sidewalk, purses swung, fake breasts bounced wildly. At the head of the pack was Nellie. As Hannah watched, she cocked back and threw something at Gavin midstride. Gavin, who stared transfixed at the women, stumbled backward as an egg hit him in the face. Another hit him on the lapel of his suit, and a third hit him dangerously close to his crotch. In seconds the women had him surrounded. They cursed at him, shouting insults.

"You never said you were married, you bastard!"

"You said I was the only one!"

"You said you'd leave your wife for me!"

"You said you loved me!"

Gavin tried to run, then stumbled and fell, finally ending up in the fetal position on the sidewalk. The barrage of insults and projectiles kept coming, though. One lady hurled rotten fruit. Another had water balloons filled with Kool-Aid. A particularly tough-looking girl who looked barely older than eighteen shot him with a paintball gun.

Hannah watched the display with a carefree smile, but eventually the sight of Gavin huddled there was just too pathetic, and she decided to have mercy on him.

"Nellie," she said.

Nellie looked at her and nodded. "All right, ladies. Fun's over," she said. At her order, the girls ceased their attack.

"Let's head over to the Hooters up the street. First pitcher is on me," Nellie declared.

A few of the women gave Gavin some final kicks, slaps, or eggs, but eventually they all followed Nellie up the street, leaving Gavin crouched in a puddle of filth. Several people had gathered around and videotaped the spectacle with their cell phones, and Hannah made a mental note to look for the video online when she got home. She had a feeling Gavin was bound for YouTube stardom.

Taking her time, Hannah sauntered up to him.

"They're gone," she said. "I don't think anyone else is going to throw anything at you."

Gavin peeked from between his fingers, then slowly got to his feet.

"Jesus . . . .What the hell just . . . ? How did they . . . ? How did you . . . ?"

Hannah smiled. "In case you decide to cheat on your next wife, a word of advice: if you're going to keep your little black book in your e-mail contacts, you might want to have a more sophisticated password than '*password.*'"

Gavin didn't seem amused. With trembling hands he swiped some of the dripping egg and paint off his face.

"And the videos. How did you... ... ?"

Hannah reached into her purse and pulled out a key on a pink, heart-shaped key ring. "When Tara was in rehab, she gave me a house key so I could feed her cats. That's one of the hazards of screwing your wife's best friend, I guess. I just walked right into her place while the two of you were out to dinner and put the cameras in her bedroom."

Gavin nodded to himself, then spit some egg onto the sidewalk.

Hannah went to leave, then turned back.

"Oh, and one more thing," she said.

Gavin winced. "What, are you going to throw something at me too?" he asked sullenly.

Hannah slipped the wedding ring off her finger. "Yes," she said, and she flicked the ring at him. He looked down at it as it clattered to the sidewalk, then picked it up, rose, and walked away, the egg in his shoes making a squishing sound with each step.

Hannah heard laughter and looked back to find Bryan behind her.

"Wow. Remind me never to cross you," he said.

She looked at him for a long moment. "You wouldn't anyway, would you?"

His eyes locked onto hers, and he didn't look away. "No," he said. "I never would." Their gaze lingered for a moment that stretched and stretched. It lasted so long, it should have been awkward, but somehow it wasn't. It was intimate. Hannah felt as if he were opening up the door of her soul and walking inside.

Finally Bryan smiled.

"So, I have a small surprise for you," he said. "I don't know if you noticed, but there was a special guest in the back of the courtroom today, cheering you on."

Bryan looked back to the courthouse steps, and Hannah followed his eye line. Bryan's brother, Sebastian, was there in a Growth House T-shirt. As soon as he saw Hannah, he ran up and gave her a big hug.

"We won! I knew it! We won!" he said, then hugged her again.

"I know! Thanks so much for coming," Hannah said, hugging him back.

Bryan smiled at them. "He was ready to testify if we needed him to, but you did a pretty good job of wrapping things up on your own."

Hannah heaved a huge sigh. After all the stress and anxiety she'd experienced over the last few months, she felt like she was breathing for the first time in ages.

"I'm just so relieved it's over!" she said. The adrenaline was going out of her system now, leaving her shaky, unsure whether she would laugh or cry.

"One more thing," Sebastian said.

Hannah looked at him, a little scared. "What now?" she asked.

Sebastian grinned. "Date my brother."

Hannah laughed, which made Sebastian laugh, which made Bryan laugh, which made Hannah laugh even harder.

She looked at Bryan. "You made him say that."

Bryan put his hands up. "No way! I didn't make him say anything. I mean, I might have *suggested* it, but I definitely didn't force him."

The laughter died down, and Bryan stepped a little closer to Hannah.

"So, what do you say?" he said, his voice soft and deep, his eyes warm, crinkled with joy, shining into hers.

She took a moment, pretending to think, making him squirm a little. "All right," she said finally. "I'll go on a date with you—on one condition . . ."

# Chapter 20

◇◇◇◇◇◇◇◇◇

Arcade video games beeped and chimed. A teenager wearing a gray mouse-head costume scampered around, posing for pictures with guests. Beau and Sage played in a big vat of colored plastic balls, rolling and frolicking and laughing, while Quinn pedantically educated Sebastian on the finer points of playing Skee-Bball—even though he was beating her by eight thousand points. Hannah and Bryan sat together at a brightly colored plastic table, talking over the remains of an extra-large cheese pizza.

"Sorry," Hannah said. "I know Chuck E. Cheese's wasn't exactly what you had in mind when you asked me out. It's just that with everything going on, I haven't had much time to spend with my kids."

Bryan smiled at her. A contagious warmth radiated from him that made her smile too. "Are you kidding?" he said. "Where else can you eat gourmet pizza, shoot hoops, and get your picture taken with a six-foot-tall mouse all under one roof?"

Hannah laughed, and with the simple release of breath and voice, she felt all the cares and stresses of the last few months melting away. If someone had told her a year ago that she would lose her husband, lose her best friend, and almost lose her company all in a matter of months and still feel capable of laughter, she'd have told them she was crazy. But here she was.

It was the end of so much: a marriage, a friendship, and a huge era of her adult life. And yet somehow it all felt like a new beginning. She was happy, she realized suddenly. Happier than she could remember ever being. The feeling was so illogical, it was scary.

But then, maybe it wasn't so illogical after all. She had built a wonderful company, she had fought for it, and she had kept it. She had survived betrayal and deceit, and found out the truth. She had destroyed the illusion that she needed Gavin—or anyone—to give her security and make her feel complete. Most of all she had discovered reserves of strength within herself that she had never known she possessed. No matter what happened now, she knew, she could face it—and overcome it.

She was not an unworthy, dependent person as Gavin, her father, and her stepmother had told her on numerous occasions. She was a shrewd businesswoman. A good mother. She was Hannah Martin. After all these years, after all her trials, she was finally, fully, truly herself. And it felt great.

"Penny for your thoughts?" Bryan asked, and she looked at him, momentarily embarrassed to realize she'd been staring off into space.

"Nothing," she said. "I'm just . . . happy."

His smiled broadened until she thought she detected the slightest bit of color in his handsome face. "Me too," he said quietly.

He reached out and took her hand, and she almost surprised herself by entwining her fingers with his.

"Hey, so I don't know if you know this about me, but I'm pretty good at some of these games," Bryan said.

"Which ones?" Hannah asked. "Foosball? Dance Dance Revolution?"

Bryan laughed. "All of the above. What do you say I try to win one of the stuffed animals hanging on the wall over behind the counter? A huge, pink teddy bear maybe. Would that impress you?"

Hannah laughed, leaning closer to him. "That's okay," she said. "But you can cheer for me while I win it myself."

www.ingramcontent.com/pod-product-compliance
Lightning Source LLC
Chambersburg PA
CBHW070458260626
47161CB00004B/1363